The Room with the Tassels

By Carolyn Wells

Originally published in 1918

The Room with the Tassels

© 2011 Resurrected Press
www.ResurrectedPress.com

Published by Resurrected Press

This classic book was handcrafted by Resurrected Press. Resurrected Press is dedicated to bringing high quality classic books back to the readers who enjoy them. These are not scanned versions of the originals, but, rather, quality checked and edited books meant to be enjoyed!

Please visit ResurrectedPress.com to view our entire catalogue!

ISBN 13: 978-1-937022-22-8

Printed in the United States of America

OTHER RESURRECTED PRESS MYSTERIES

By Carolyn Wells
Raspberry Jam
The Man Who Fell Through the Earth
In The Onyx Lobby
Vicky Van

By Louis Tracy
The Strange Case of Mortimer Fenley
The Albert Gate Mystery
The Stowmarket Mystery

By J. S. Fletcher
The Orange-Yellow Diamond
The Middle Temple Murder

By A. A. Milne
The Red House Mystery

By Agatha Christie
The Mysterious Affair at Styles

By Arthur Griffiths
The Passenger from Calais
The Rome Express

From the Dr. John Thorndyke Series
By R. Austin Freeman
The Red Thumb Mark
The Eye of Osiris
The Mystery of 31 New Inn
John Thorndyke's Cases
The Cat's Eye

By Arthur J. Rees
The Hampstead Mystery
The Mystery of the Downs

Visit RessurectedPress.com to see our entire catalog.

FOREWORD

In *The Room with the Tassels* Carolyn Wells gives the reader as supernatural thriller in which a group of wealthy New Yorkers decide to spend a summer month investigating the supernatural in a haunted mansion set deep in the woods of the Vermont's Green Mountains. The mansion comes complete with the legend of a woman who murdered her husband in the so called "room with the tassels" and the group finds themselves confronted with various apparitions and unexplained events. The plot, with the remote abandoned house, creepy landlord and psychic warnings, plays like the prototype for every episode of "Scooby-Doo" until two members of the party meet their death. Were the deaths the result of supernatural forces, or were they murder?

The supernatural and spiritualism (the belief in contact with the dead) were topics that appeared in numerous mysteries of the period including several by Wells herself. Spiritualism, which has a long history both in America and Britain was undergoing one of its periodic revivals at the time the novel was written. A number of well known public figures including several prominent scientists were interested in the subject and conducted personal investigations. Whether believers or not, contemporary readers found the subject intensely interesting and these mysteries were quite popular.

The Room with the Tassels features the second of Wells' detectives, Pennington Wise, Fleming Stone being the first. Both were to appear in a number of mysteries in the 1910's and 20's. Whereas Stone is described as a dignified man in his early fifties, Pennington Wise is an artist in his thirties and has a more relaxed and informal manner, though he takes his detection seriously. At work, he is always accompanied by a young woman, Zizi, who is as much a mystery as the cases they are involved with. Both detectives are renowned for their abilities to solve the toughest cases.

The novel, as with many of Wells' mysteries, takes on an architectural aspect. The mansion, with its stout bronze doors, marble façade, and numerous locks would seem impregnable for human intrusion. Even the closest examination fails to reveal a secret passage or hidden entrance, yet such an entrance must exist if the various supernatural manifestations are caused by human hands and not real, and much of the novel is concerned with resolving this question.

Much of the book deals with the interplay of the various characters as they deal with the fact that the supernatural may actually be real. Wells' strong point as a writer is with portraying realistically the upper middle class characters that populate her novels and the way they confront various contemporary issues. *The Room with the Tassels* is no exception and is one of her better efforts in this regard.

Resurrected Press is happy to bring its readers this new edition of *The Room with the Tassels*. We hope that you will find it both enjoyable and entertaining.

About the Author

Carolyn Wells, June 18, 1862 - March 26, 1942 was an American writer and poet. She was best known for her books of poetry and humor until around 1910 she read one of Anna Katherine Green's mysteries and took up the genre. Many of her mysteries featured the detective Fleming Stone. She was married to Hadwin Houghton, heir to the Houghton-Mifflin publishing company. She was a collector of poetry by other authors, and, upon her death, she bequeathed her collection of the works of Walt Witman to the Library of Congress.

Greg Fowlkes
Editor-In-Chief
Resurrected Press
www.ResurrectedPress.com

Table of Contents

WITH LOVE AND HOMAGE

This Book is Dedicated
to

HATTIE BELLE JOHNSTON

CHAPTER 1: WANTED: A HAUNTED HOUSE

"BUT I know it's so,—for Mrs. Fairbanks saw it herself,—and heard it, too!"

The air of finality in the gaze levelled at Braye defied contradiction, so he merely smiled at the girl who was doing the talking. But, talking or silent, Eve Carnforth was well worth smiling at. Her red hair was of that thin, silky, flat lying sort, that spells temper, but looks lovely, and her white, delicate skin,—perhaps the least bit hand painted,—showed temperament while her eyes, of the colour called beryl,—whatever that is,—showed all sorts of things.

Then from her canna hued lips fell more wisdom. "And Professor Hardwick believes it, too, and he's—"

"A college professor," broke in Landon, "don't try to gild his refinement! But really, Eve, you mustn't believe in spooks,—it isn't done—"

"Oh, but it is! You've no idea how many people,—scientific and talented people,—are leaning toward spiritualism just now. Why, Sir Oliver Lodge says that after the war great and powerful assistance will be given by spirit helpers in matters of reconstruction and great problems of science."

Milly Landon's laugh rang out, and she politely clapped a little, fat hand over her mouth to stifle it.

Milly Landon was an inveterate giggler, but don't let that prejudice you against her. She was the nicest, dearest dumpling of a little woman who ever giggled her way through life. And as hostess on this present Sunday afternoon occasion, she sat, one foot tucked under her, on the davenport in her long, narrow parlour, on one of New York's East Seventieth streets.

It was a parlour like thousands of others in the city, and the quartette of people talking there were much like the people talking in those other parlours, that Sunday afternoon. Their only superiority lay in the fact that they constitute part of the personnel of this absorbing tale, and the other people do not.

Milly and her very satisfactory husband, Wynne Landon, were affably entertaining Rudolph Braye and the herein before described Eve Carnforth, two pleasing callers, and the talk had turned on psychological matters and then, by inevitable stages, to the supernatural and spiritualism.

"It is all coming in again," Eve declared, earnestly. "You know it was taken very seriously about thirty or forty years ago, and then because of fake mediums and fraudulent seances, it fell into disrepute. But now, it's being taken up in earnest, and I, for one, am terribly interested."

"But it's so old fashioned, Eve," and Milly looked at her guest in disdain.

"It's gammon and spinach, that's what it is," declared Landon, "very rubbishy gammon and a poor quality of spinach!"

"Queen Victoria didn't think so," Eve informed them. "She may have been old fashioned, but she believed thoroughly in the spiritual reappearance of her friends who died, and especially took comfort in the communion and visitation of her dead husband."

"It's this way, I think," offered Braye; "it seems to me it's like that old 'Lady or the Tiger' story, you believe or not, according to your character or disposition. You know, it depended on your own nature, whether you think the Lady came out of the door, or the Tiger. And so with spooks, if you want to believe in them, you do."

"Don't say spooks, please," begged Eve; "say phantasms, or even ghosts."

"Is that the usage in the best mediumistic circles?" and Braye smiled. "Well, I think I could more easily believe in a spook than a phantasm. The latter sounds so unreal, but a good honest Injun spook seems sort of plausible."

"They're all unreal," began Landon, but Eve interrupted. "They're not unreal, Wynne; they're immaterial, of course, but that isn't being unreal. You have a real soul, haven't you, although it is immaterial? and I suppose you don't call your mind material, even if your brain is."

"Now you're quibbling, Eve," and Landon grew a bit more serious. "When I say unreal, I mean imperceptible to the senses. I hold that a departed spirit cannot return to earth and be seen, heard, or felt by mortal human beings. All the stories of such things to the contrary notwithstanding. If you or any one else has power to show me a visible spook,—I beg pardon, phantasm,—I'll be glad to see it, but I'm from Missouri. I wouldn't be a bit afraid of it, but I'd have to be jolly well convinced of its integrity. No faked up spectres would go down with me!"

"But how can you know?" asked Milly. "I'd be scared to death of one, I'm sure, but if Wynne wants to see one, I do. Let's all go to a seance, or whatever they call the things. Shall us?"

"No, indeed!" cried Eve. "Professional seances are always fakes. And I don't aspire to *see* one. If we could get some messages from the beyond, that would satisfy me."

"Get messages how?" asked Braye.

"Oh, by a Ouija board, or some such way."

"Ouija!" derided Landon; "that's the biggest fraud of all!"

"Only in the hands of frauds. If we tried it here by ourselves and if we all trusted each other not to stoop to deception of any sort that would be a fair test."

"I'd like that," and Milly giggled in pleased anticipation. "That wouldn't frighten me, and I'd promise to play fair."

"There'd be no reason for not playing fair," said Eve, seriously. "We're not a pack of silly children who want to trick one another. If we could get together some evening and have an earnest, serious test, I'd agree. But not if there's to be the least suspicion of anybody trying trickery."

At this point two more callers arrived, and Milly jumped up to greet them.

"Mr. Bruce!" she exclaimed, "how nice to see you! And Vernie,—my goodness, how you've grown!"

"Indeed, yes," and Vernie Reid, a most lively and energetic sub deb of sixteen, darted from one to another, greeting all with interest.

"Hello, Cousin Rudolph, what are you doing here? Mooning after Miss Carnforth, I s'pose. Dear Mrs. Landon, let me sit here by you. I want to show you my graduating gifts."

"Oh, yes, you've just had commencement, haven't you?"

"Yes, and Uncle Gifford gave me this heavenly wrist watch, and my respected Cousin Rudolph, over there, sent me this pendant. Isn't it stunning? Oh, I had beautiful presents. I'd like to graduate every year!"

"Aren't you going to school any more at all?"

"Dunno yet. Uncle Gifford says I am, I say I'm not. It remains to be seen. Though I don't mind confiding to you that I usually get my own way. And, too, out in Chicago, you know, we're not such terrible highbrows. Something tells me my schooldays are over. I think Uncle Gif needs the pleasure of my society at home. And, too, I want to get acquainted with Cousin Rudolph. Until this week I haven't seen him for years."

"He isn't your cousin, Vernie."

"Same as. He's a son of Uncle Gif's half-brother, and I'm a daughter of Uncle's own sister, so it sort of evens up. Anyway, I like Cousin Rudolph, because he's such a good looking young man, and he's promised to take me round New York some. That's why I'm so jealous of Miss Carnforth or any other girl."

Vernie was so pretty that her chatter amused the whole crowd. She was brown haired and brown eyed, and somewhat of a browned complexion, by reason of much tennis and outdoor life at the school from which she had just been graduated. And after a summer spent among the Eastern resorts, she and her Uncle were to return to their Chicago home, where they had lived all of Vernie's orphaned life. Gifford Bruce idolized the girl and though often short and crabbed in his manner to others, he was never cross or stern to his dead sister's child.

"What were you talking about when we came in?" Vernie asked, smiling at Milly. "You were all so in earnest, it must have been something important."

"Of ghosts," answered Braye, looking at the pretty child. "Do you enjoy them?"

"Oh, don't I!" cried Vernie. "Why, at school we just ate 'em up! Table tippings and all such things, as soon as lights were out!"

"We don't mean that sort," said Eve. "We were talking seriously."

"Count me out, then," laughed Vernie. "Our ghosts weren't a bit real. I did most of 'em myself, jogging the table, when the others didn't know it!"

Eve's scarlet lips came together in a narrow line, but the others laughed at the Vernie as she babbled on.

"Yes, and we tried the Ouija board. I can make it say anything I want to."

"Good for you, Kiddie," cried Braye, "I believe I like your notion of these things better than the ideas of the psychologists. It sounds a lot more fun!"

"And comes nearer the truth," declared Mr. Bruce. "I've looked up these matters and I've read all the best and most authoritative books on the subjects. There are many writers more diffuse and circumstantial, but Andrew Lang sums up the whole situation in his able way. He says there are no ghosts, but there are hallucinations. And that explains all."

"It doesn't to me," and Eve's beryl eyes took on a mystic, faraway look. "I, too, have read a lot of books—"

"Scientific or psychic?" interrupted Mr. Bruce, acidly.

"Psychical and Theosophic—"

"Rubbish! The Theosophic bunch have been in the discard for years."

"That's what I say," put in Milly, "the whole business is old fashioned."

"It isn't a question of fashion," and Gifford Bruce spoke assuredly; "the subject is one that recurs in waves, as many such things do. Why, there have been ghosts and haunted houses in people's imagination ever since there has been man and a house for him to live in. Some are spoken of in the Bible, the primitive Australians had legions of ghosts, the awful Dyaks record them, and there is scarce a castle or palace of the middle ages that hasn't its Woman in White, or a Little Gray Lady or the Man in Black. And in an old Egyptian papyrus, there's an account of a defunct lady who insisted on haunting her husband to his great distaste."

"My goodness, Uncle Gif, you do know a lot about it!" and Vernie went over and sat on the arm of his chair. "Tell us more. I like this sort of ghost stories better than the fool stunts we did at school."

"I'm not telling ghost stories, child, I'm only declaring that ghost stories are merely *stories*, and in no case a true relation of happenings. Lang investigated thousands of cases, and in ten out of every eleven, he states, fraud was proved."

"Quite so," said Eve, "and it is that eleventh case that interests the real thinker, the true inquirer."

"But the eleventh case was simply not proven, it never has been shown that it was really a ghostly visitation."

"But they do say, Uncle Gifford," observed Braye, "that the very fact of the frauds being perpetrated proves that there was something to imitate. If no spirit had ever returned to earth and made itself manifest, no one would have thought of pretending that one did."

"Nonsense and super nonsense! Why, Rudolph, perpetual motion is not a real thing, but how many times has it been pretended! You don't remember the Keeley Motor, but that deceived thousands into believing that perpetual motion was at last discovered, but it wasn't; and that fraud doesn't prove that perpetual motion, without adequate cause, exists."

"Here comes Professor Hardwick," exclaimed Milly, "splendid to have him come just now! Sit down, Professor, and get right into the game. You know all these people, except this angel child, Miss Vernie Reid."

"I am an angel," declared Vernie, "but I'm no child! I've just graduated with honours and diplomas and lots of presents. Now, I'm out in the great world, and glory, but I love it! But don't mind me, Professor, go right on and tell us all you know about ghosts and ghostesses."

"Bless my soul! I don't know anything about them."

"Well, do you believe in ghosts?"

"What do you mean by ghosts? How do you define a ghost?"

"Ah, there's the rub," said Landon. "These people are all talking at cross purposes. Mr. Bruce means a scarecrow phantom rigged up in sheets, Miss Carnforth means a supernatural being of some sort, but I take a ghost, in the proper sense, to mean the visible soul of some one who has died."

"What do you mean by visible soul? Disembodied?"

"No," considered Landon, "I suppose I mean clothed in a body,—that is an apparent body."

"And raiment?" asked the old Professor.

"Yes, certainly. I never heard of a nude spook!"

"Then your visible soul is concealed by a body of flesh, and clothes, of fabric, or, at least, apparently so. The soul, I take it, would show but low visibility."

"Good, Hardwick!" cried Mr. Bruce. "Give them a jolt, they need it,—talking such rubbish!"

"Rubbish, Bruce? What do you mean by rubbish?"

"Why, all this ghost gabble—"

"How do you know it's rubbish? Have you personally disproved it? Do you mean intentional rubbish? Are they talking deceptively, or are they themselves deceived?"

"By the Lord Harry, Hardwick, I had forgotten you were such a stickler for words! I must choose my diction carefully. Do you, then, believe that so-called supernatural appearances are caused by psychical influences or are hallucinations of the senses? There, I think I've put it clearly."

"Fairly so. But I can't answer clearly. I never express an opinion on a grave question—"

Milly's hand flew up to her mouth to repress an involuntary giggle. "A *grave* question!" she exploded. "It surely is."

The Professor looked at her thoughtfully. "It is," he went on, "and it is no laughing matter. As I was saying, I never state an opinion without being sure of my facts. Now, I've had no experience, personally, with supernatural matters, and so am unfit to discuss them. But, I admit I should be very glad to have some such experience. Yes, I certainly should."

"Really," and Eve Carn forth looked interested. "I can arrange it for you, Professor Hardwick."

"No, no, my dear lady, I do not mean that I want to go to a seance, where the so called medium throws flowers and things out of a cabinet, or toots trumpets and bangs cymbals! No, thank you, I've seen such often."

"What would you choose as an experience?" asked Landon.

"I'd like to go to a house that is reputed haunted, and in circumstances that preclude all possibility of fraud, see the haunting spirits or hear them, for myself."

"Me, too!" cried Vernie. "Oh, I do think that would be the rippingest fun! If you ever do it, Professor, mayn't I go with you?"

"I'll go along." said Eve. "Wouldn't that be a splendid proof! To have such a scientific and open minded man as the Professor, and a few others who are in earnest and anxious to learn. You couldn't go, Mr. Bruce. You are too sceptical."

"I'm just the one you need," he laughed. "A balance wheel to keep you enthusiasts straight. But haunted houses are not to be found on every bush in America. If we were in England now,—or Scotland."

"They do have some over here," Landon asserted. "I read of one recently, and I've heard of others."

"Let's find one," suggested Eve, "and spend our summer vacation in it! Wouldn't that be a lark?"

"Oh, do!" exclaimed Vernie. "I'd just love it! May I go, Uncle Gifford? Oh, please let me."

"Only if I go myself, child. The spooks,—I beg their pardon, phantasms, might carry you off. I'll have to go along to rescue you."

"Phantasms don't carry people off," said Eve, contemptuously. "And though I'd like to consider this plan, I'd only do so, if we were all in earnest as investigators, whatever our opinions may be."

"Come on, let's go," said Landon. "I think it a great little old scheme. Make up a party, you know, but every one who joins must promise to be earnest and honest. Must promise to do nothing to fool or mislead the others, but keep a fair and open mind for any developments. Of course, there won't be any developments, but we can have a jolly time and we can have wild discussions."

"Wynne would rather have a discussion than eat," said his wife. "I'll go, and I'll be the housekeeper and chaperon of the crowd, if, as Wynne says, there'll be no developments. I'd love the outing, and I think this a splendid party to belong to. And let's take Norma Cameron. She's a sensitive, or whatever you call it, and she'll help you out, Eve."

"Why make the party any larger?" asked Eve, a little petulantly. "The crowd here now seems just right and congenial and all that."

"Why lug in Norma?" said Braye, smiling. "I don't know said Norma, but I agree with Eve that the party here is just sort of complete."

"Yes, I will take Norma. The poor child never gets an outing, and she'd just love this chance."

"You talk as if we were going to a summer resort," said Landon. "In the first place, Milly, I doubt if we can find a properly haunted house in a pleasant locality, that is for rent."

"Of course we can't," declared Mr. Bruce. "The whole scheme is idiotic. But if you can work it out, Landon, I'll go along, and take this little piece of property." He looked smilingly at the eager eyed Vernie. "She's due for some fun after her school work, and if she likes this stunt, let's try to put it over."

"How would you set out to find a house?" asked Braye.

"Advertise," said Landon, promptly. "I know a firm of real estate agents, that I'll bet could manage it in short order. Say we try it?"

"I'm going to take Norma," .insisted Milly. "Mayn't I, Wynne?"

"Take anything or anybody you wish, my cherished one. But then, oughtn't we to have another man?"

"Yes," said Milly, decidedly. "I hate a bunch of hens, without plenty of menfolks about. Who knows a nice, good natured, all round adaptable dinner man?"

"I know just the chap," said Braye, "but he's a minister. Or, at least, he used to be. But he's an awfully good fellow, and most agreeable parlour company."

"What's his name?" asked Landon.

"Tracy. I met him first in Chicago, some years ago, and I've always liked him."

"All right, if Milly asks Norma, you ask your friend, but it's a case of first catch your house!"

"It's got to be a nice house, and fairly comfortable," Milly stipulated, "or I won't go."

"It's got to have a well authenticated ghost, or I won't go," laughed Braye. "I don't believe in the things, but I'd like to have a chance to hear their clanking chains, or whatever they perform on."

"I'll go just for the fun of the thing," said Vernie, "and if we do catch a ghost, so much the better!"

Chapter 2: The Old Montgomery Place

At the Fisher and Hibbard Real Estate and Country House Agency, Wayne Landon had a spirited interview with their Mr. Fisher, and finally induced that somewhat unwilling gentleman to advertise for a haunted house.

"It's a purely business matter," Landon argued, "and if you're any sort of a live agency you ought to do your best to get for your clients any such peculiar domiciles as they may desire."

"I understand that," patiently explained Mr. Fisher, "but it's such a crazy thing to do. How would a dignified firm like ours look advertising for a house warranted haunted?"

"Don't use your own firm name, then. Have answers sent to a fictitious address. Oh, you can manage it, Fisher. I don't mean you can surely get one, but you can manage to try. And if the house is pleasant and attractive, it doesn't matter, between you and me, if there isn't any ghost, after all. But I want a *bona fide* story. I mean, I don't want a house that the owner pretends is haunted, just so he can rent it. It must be a well known legend or ghost story connected with the place."

"There are plenty of such," and Fisher laughed. "I've struck them occasionally, and because of that well authenticated story, known to all the neighbours, I couldn't rent them. To have one asked for is a new experience here."

"Well, I've told you the whole state of the case. You see why we want it, and though the ghost part is the primary factor with some of us, my wife and I care more about a pleasant setting for a month's house party."

Landon's personality went far toward gaining his end, and Mr. Fisher promised to do what he could. As a lawyer of fine standing, and a man of ample means, Wynne Landon was a desirable man to please, and the order was taken.

And when, a few weeks later, word came that a possible opportunity had offered, Landon telephoned for Braye to go with him, and they went to investigate it at once.

"It's this way," said Mr. Fisher to the listening men. "There's a big house up in Vermont,—in the Green Mountain region, not so very far from Manchester. But it's a lonely locality, quite high up, and near a lake."

"Sounds fine so far," commented Landon; "go on."

"A man named Stebbins is the owner. I haven't seen him, but here's his letter. Read it, you'll get the idea better than I can tell you." So they read:

"FISHER AND HIBBARD :
"Dear sirs:
"I've got a house, and it sure is haunted. It's up here in the mountains, and it's a good house, and a big one, but in some disrepair. Leastways, things is old fashioned, and not, as you may say, up to date. But nothing ornery. All high toned and proper, only old and somewhat wore out. It's the old Montgomery mansion, built along about 1700 and something. But it's been added to since, and it's a sort of mixed up architecture. About forty rooms into it, I should judge, though I ain't never counted them. And most of them haunted. But they ain't no use going into particulars unless somebody really wants to rent it. I've tried nineteen years, and nobody'll take it, cause it's so lonesome like. It's called Black Aspens, mostly I guess, cause the thick groves of aspen trees all around look black at night, and Lord knows it's a fit place for ghosts. Anyway it's haunted and I can swear to that. But the story of the haunt I won't set down until I hear from you again. But you can take my affydavy it's a real haunt and there's a real reason for it.
"Yours truly,

"ELIJAH STEBBINS."

"Sounds good to me; what do you think, Rudolph?" said Landon.

"All right, if it's genuine. Some of us ought to go up there and size it up before the whole crowd goes. Think so?"

"Yes, unless we can get a photograph, or some sort of a plan of the place. And, you know, Braye, I don't care such a lot about a ghost, if we can get a good intelligent crowd of people together. That's the only sort of vacation I care for. I wouldn't give a picayune for a month in a big summer hotel, or a little summer boarding house, where you may meet good talkers and you may not. But with Eve Carnforth and Norma Cameron and the Professor and, pardon the bouquet, you, I foresee some good old chin chins. And, add to this, picturesque, even wild mountain scenery, I somehow think we're in for a good time."

"I agree. Wish Uncle Gif and Vernie weren't going, though. He's a dictatorial old chap, though a good sport, and as to Vernie, I don't think it's the right place for a flapper."

"Oh, it won't hurt the kiddie. She's a mighty sensible little piece and she's ready to eat up experiences. She may as well be with her own people."

"That's just it. She's lived nearly all her life alone with Uncle, and he isn't enough people for her. She ought to have a woman to look after her, now she's out of school."

"Well, what's the matter with Milly? For this trip at least. Milly loves the little girl, and will have a good influence over her."

"That's right as rain, but I'm not sure Eve Carnforth is desirable company for Vernie."

"Oh, Eve isn't a bad sort. And with her strict Uncle, and you and Milly and me to look after the child, Eve can't do much to counteract."

"She probably won't do anything. It's all right, Wynne. Now shall we decide to take this Montgomery place?"

"Oh, no, we can't decide positively. I'm pretty sure we shall take it, but I think we ought to call a confab of the whole bunch to discuss it."

Meantime, Eve Carnforth was talking it over with Milly Landon.

"I adore the plan," Eve said,"except your insistence on taking Norma Cameron. I don't like her, Milly, and you know it."

"Now, Eve, cunnin' little cherub child, don't let the greeny weeny eyed monster claim you for his own! You know perf'ly well," Milly giggled, "that you don't want Norma along, because you think she will attract Friend Braye."

"Why, Milly Landon! What nonsense! I don't care two cents for Rudolph Braye—"

"Oh, I don't mean romantically, but I do know you want to be top of the psychic heap, up there, and you think little Norma will get ahead of you in phantasmagoria, or whatever you call it."

"No, it isn't that; but Norma does think she knows it all, and she puts on such airs about her clairvoyance, and calls herself a sensitive and all that."

"Well, let her. You can hold your own; and, too, Eve, if we carry out this scheme, I think we ought all to pull together, and help each other. And we can't do that, if there's antagonism or rivalry. Now, can we? And if you're in earnest, as you've always insisted you are, you ought to be glad of any help Norma can give. She feels that way about you. When I asked her to go, she was delighted that you were to be in the party, because, she said, you were so interested and so well up in all these things we're going to discover."

"I suppose I am silly. I may as well confess I'm not sure of Norma. She wouldn't be above pretending she heard or saw things, even if she didn't."

"Fiddlesticks! There won't be any pretending! Or, if there is, it'll be discovered right straight off. Why, Wynne is terribly in earnest,—about having it all fair and square, I mean,—and so is the Professor, and I'd like to see any one fool Gifford Bruce! And little Vernie is a real wideawake. There won't be anything doing that that child doesn't know, if it's fraud or foolery! Don't you believe it, my dear. Norma Cameron won't pull any wool over anybody's eyes in our party. No, siree!"

The crowd came together that night to discuss the house that had been offered, and to come to a decision.

Norma Cameron was present, and her manner and appearance were so exactly opposite to those of Eve Carn forth, that it was small wonder the girls were not congenial.

Norma was blonde, and had what her friends called a seraphic countenance and her enemies, a doll face. For Norma had enemies. She was prominent in war relief work and public charities of many kinds, and it is seldom possible for such a one to go through the world entirely peaceably. But all conceded that her doll face was a very pretty one, and few who criticized it, would not have been glad to wear it.

Her golden hair was softly curly, and her sky blue eyes big and expressive. But her complexion was her greatest beauty; soft as a rose petal, the pink and white were so delicately blended as to make a new observer suspect art's assistance. A second glance, however, removed all such suspicion, for no hare's foot could ever have produced that degree of perfection. Her softly rounded chin, and creamy throat were exquisitely moulded, and her usual expression was gentle and amiable.

But Norma was no namby pamby character, and her eyes could turn to deep violet, and her pink cheeks flush rosily if she ran up against unjustice or meanness. That was why her career of philanthropy was not always a serene path, for she never hesitated to speak her mind and her mind was of a positive type.

Always outspoken, though, was Norma. No slyness or deceit marked her procedure, never did she say behind any one's back what she would not say to his face.

And this was the principal reason why Norma and Eve could never hit it off. For Eve frequently carried tales, and sometimes denied them later. Milly, however, was friends with both girls, and secretly hoped that if they could all get away together, the two warring natures might react on each other for good. Then, too, both were immensely interested in psychics, and if they were rivals in this field, so much better chance for all concerned, to find out the things they were to look for.

"I think," said Norma, at the confab, "it would be better for two of the crowd, say, Mr. and Mrs. Landon, to go up first and look at the house. It sounds fine, but it may be impossible. So, why get us all up there, only to come home again?"

"I don't think so," said Eve, promptly, while Milly giggled to hear the two begin to disagree at once. "I think it would be a lot more fun for us all to go and see it for the first time together. Then, if it isn't livable, we can all come back, but we shall have had a sort of picnic out of it, at least."

"Yes, I think that, too!" put in Vernie, who was beside herself with joy at the outlook. "Oh, what a gorgeous party it will be! Do we go in the train, or motors or what?"

"Hush, Vernie," said her Uncle, "we haven't decided to go at all, yet. Where is this place, Landon?"

"The post office is East Dryden. The house is about a mile further up the mountain. I fancy it's a picturesque sort of a place, though with few modern appointments. Fisher got a little more data, somehow, and he says it's a hodge podge old pile, as to architecture, as it's been rebuilt, or added to several times. But I don't care about all that, I mean, if we don't like the appointments we needn't stay. What I want is the ghost story. Shall we send to Stebbins for that before we take the place, or go on a wild goose chase entirely?"

"Oh, let's start off without knowing anything about it," and old Mr. Bruce's eyes twinkled like a boy's at thought of an escapade.

"Good for you, Uncle!" and Vernie shouted with glee. "I didn't know you were such an old top, did you, Cousin Rudolph?"

"Well, I've known him longer than you have, Flapper, and I'm not so surprised at his wanting a sporting proposition. But, I say, Milly, if we're going to take Tracy, you people ought to see him and give him the once over first. Maybe you won't like him at all."

"Oh, your friends are sure to be our friends, Rudolph," said Landon, "but telephone him to run up here, can't you? It's only fair to let him in on the planning."

Tracy came, and he made good at once. His ministerial air was softened by a charming smile and a certain chivalry of address that pleased the women and satisfied the men.

"What about servants?" he asked, after the main details had been explained to him.

"That's what I'm thinking about," said Milly. "I don't want to take our servants, they'd be scared to death in such a place, and, too, we can't go ghost hunting under Charles' nose! He'd sniff at us!"

"Right you are!" agreed Landon. "Charles is one estimable and valuable butler, but he's no sort to take on the picnic we're out for."

"Don't let's take any servants," suggested Eve, "but get some up there. Natives, you know."

"That would be better," said Mr. Bruce. "Then, they'll be used to the place, and can tell us of the legends and traditions, you see."

"You're poking fun," said Eve, reproachfully, "but it's true, all the same. Do we go in motors?"

"I think so," said Landon. "Two big cars would take us all, and we can leave our luggage to be sent up if we stay."

"Of course we'll stay," asserted Milly. "I love that old house already, and if there's no ghost at all. I'll be just as well pleased, and I'll stay the month out, with whoever wants to stay with me."

"I'll stand by you," said Norma, "and I'll own up that I don't really expect any spectral manifestations up there, anyway."

"It matters little what you expect," and Professor Hardwick looked at her thoughtfully. "We're going investigating, not expecting."

"Don't you expect anything, Prof?" asked Vernie, gaily.

"What do you mean by expect, child? Do you mean wish or think?"

"Gracious, goodness, Professor I—I never know what I mean by the words I use, and I never care!"

Professor Hardwick's hobby was the use of words, and rarely did he fail to question it, if a word was misused or uncertainly used in his presence. But he smiled benignly on the pretty child, and didn't bother her further.

Finally, the men drew together to make up the budget of necessary expenses and the women talked clothes.

"Smocks all round," said Norma, who loved the unconventional in dress.

"Not for me!" said Eve, who didn't.

Milly giggled. "Let every one wear just what she chooses," she settled it. "I'm at my best in white linen in the summer time, but what about laundry? Well, I shall leave two sets of things packed, and then send for whichever I want."

Norma, uninterested in clothes, edged over toward the men. Though a friend of the Landons and acquainted with Professor Hardwick, she had never met Braye or Tracy before.

Both succumbed to her sure fire smile, but Tracy showed it and Braye didn't.

"Sit here, Miss Cameron," and Tracy eagerly made a place for her at his side; "we need a lady assistant. How much do you think it ought to cost to provision nine people and two or three natives for a month?"

"It isn't a question of what it ought to cost," returned Norma, "but what it will cost. But in any case it will be less than most of us would spend if we went to the average summer hotel. So why not just put down some round numbers, divide 'em by nine and let it go at that?"

"Fine!" approved Landon. "No food dictator could beat that scheme! I wonder if ghost hunters are as hungry as other hunters, or if we'll be so scared we'll lose our appetites."

"I have a profound belief in ghosts," Norma asserted, "but I shall only indulge in it between meals. Count me in for all the good things going, three times a day."

"What do you mean by profound?" asked the Professor; "deep seated or widely informed?"

"Both," answered Norma, flashing her pretty smile at the serious old man. "Profundity of all kinds is my happy hunting ground, and on this trip I expect to get all the profundity I want."

"And I'm the girl to put the fun in profundity," cried Vernie, coming over to them. "My mission is to keep you serious people joyed up. Mr. Tracy, your profession won't interfere with your having a jolly time, will it? No, I see it won't, by that twinkly little smile."

"You may count on me," said the clergyman a bit stiffly, but with a cordial glance at the girl.

"And I can wind Professor Hardwick round my finger," Vernie went on, "for a companion on a gay lark, I don't know any one better than a dry as dust old college professor!"

The object of this encomium received it with a benignant smile, but Gifford Bruce reproved his saucy niece.

"I'll leave you at home, miss, if you talk impertinences," he declared.

"Not much you won't, my bestest, belovedest Uncle! Why, I'm the leading lady of this troupe. And I expect the spectre will appear to me first of all. That's my motto: 'Spect the Spectre! How's that? Then the rest of you can inspect the spectre!"

"Vernie! don't be so excruciatingly funny," begged Braye, while Milly Landon giggled at the pretty child, whose charm and sweetness took all rudeness from her foolery.

"Perhaps we ought to call in an inspector to inspect the spectre," contributed Landon.

"There, there, Wynne," said Braye, "we'll take such stuff from an ignorant little girl but not from a grown up man."

"Ignorant, huh!" scorned Vernie. "I'll bet you couldn't have passed my examination in psychology!"

"Perhaps not," admitted Braye, "but after this trip of ours, we'll all be honour men."

"I want it thoroughly understood," said Mr. Bruce, "that I range myself on the side of the sceptics. I don't want to sail under false colours and I wish to state positively that there are no ghosts or phantasms or any such things. Moreover, I announce my intention of fooling you gullible ones, if I can."

"Oh, that isn't fair!" exclaimed Landon. "I don't believe in the things either, but I want an honest test. Why, you take away the whole point of the experiment if you're going to put up a trick onus!"

"No, no, Bruce," said the Professor, "that won't do. Come, now, give me your word there'll be no hocus pocus or I refuse to go at all."

"If it's any sort of a real test, Hardwick, it oughtn't to be possible to fool you."

"That's true," said Eve; "and I'm not afraid of any tricks. If they are tricks, I'll know it—"

"I too," said Norma. "I'm sensitive to all psychical manifestations and if I can't tell a real phantasm from Mr. Bruce's tricks, I deserve to be fooled."

"I think it's a good thing that Mr. Bruce warned us," observed John Tracy. "It puts us on our guard. But I think the rest of us ought to agree not to do anything of that sort. We can expect and discount Mr. Bruce's little game, but if others are going to do the same, it seems to me the game isn't worth playing."

"Right you are!" declared Landon, and forthwith everybody present except Gifford Bruce solemnly pledged his or her word to do nothing tricky or fraudulent, and to preserve an open-minded, honest attitude toward any developments they might experience.

"And with eight argus eyed inquirers watching him, Mr. Bruce can't put anything over," opined Landon, and the others agreed.

CHAPTER 3: BLACK ASPENS

THOUGH mid July, it was a chilly dusk through which the two motor cars ascended the last stretch of mountain road toward the old Montgomery mansion. The sun set early behind the Green Mountains and the house, half way up an eastern slope, appeared faintly through the Shadows.

To the right, tall forest trees waved their topmost branches with an eerie, soughing sound, or stood, menacingly silent, in black, sullen majesty. Beneath them a tangled underbrush gave forth faint, rustling hints of some wild life or suddenly ceased to a grim stillness.

Then the road lay through a thick grove of aspens, close, black and shivering as they stood, sentinel like and fearsome, only dimly outlined against the dark, clouded sky. Once in the grove, the shadows were dense, and the quivering sounds seemed intensified to a muttered protest against intrusion. A strange bird gave forth a few raucous notes, and then the dread silence returned.

A quick, damp chill foreboded still water and the road followed the margin of a small lake or pond, sinister in its inky depths, which mirrored the still blacker aspen trees.

Suddenly, in a small clearing, they came upon the house. In the uncertain light it seemed enormous, shapeless and beyond all words repelling. It seemed to have a personality, defiant and forbidding, that warned of mystery and disaster. Aspen trees, tall and gaunt, grew so close that their whispering leaves brushed the windows, and crowded in protecting, huddled clumps to ward off trespassers.

No lights showed through the deep caverns of the windows, but one faint gleam flickered above the entrance door.

"Whew!" cried Landon, jumping from his seat with a thud on the stone terrace, "I won't go through that woods again! I'll go home in an aeroplane,—and I'm ready to go now!"

"So am I," said Milly, in a quivering, tearful voice. "Oh, Wynne, why did we ever come?"

"Now, now," cheered Braye, "keep your heads, it's all right. Only these confounded shadows make it impossible to know just where we're at. Here's the house, and by jinks, it's built of marble!"

"Of course," said the Professor, who was curiously feeling of the old ivy grown stone, "this is the marble country, you know. Vermont marble was plenty enough when this house was put up."

"Let's get in," begged Vernie. "It isn't as much fun as I thought it would be."

They went, in a close group, up a short flight of broad marble steps and reached a wide portico, in the centre of which was a spacious vestibule indented into the building, and which stood within the main wall. Though the walls of the house were of marble, those of this vestibule were of panelled mahogany, and the entrance doorway was flanked on either side by large bronze columns, which stood half within and half without the mahogany wall.

"Some house!" exclaimed Tracy, in admiration of the beautiful details, which though worn and blackened by time, were of antique grandeur.

"These bronze doors must have come from Italy. They're marvellous. I'm glad I came."

"Oh, do get in, Wynne," wailed Milly. "You can examine the house to morrow. I wish we hadn't come!"

Landon was about to make search for knocker or bell, when one of the big bronze doors swung open, and a man peered out.

"You folks here?" he said, a bit unnecessarily. "Bring another lamp, Hester."

"Yes, we're here," Landon assured him, "and we want to get in out of the wet!"

"Rainin'?" and the man stepped out of the door to look, blocking all ingress.

"No! that's a figure of speech!" Landon's nerves were on edge. "Open that door,—the other one,—let us in!"

"Go on in, who's henderin' you?" and the indifferent host stepped out of the way.

Landon went in first and Braye followed, as the others crowded after. At first they could see only a gloomy cavernous hall, its darkness accentuated by one small lamp on a table.

"Thought I wouldn't light up till you got here," and the man who had admitted them came in and closed the door. "I'm Stebbins, and here's the keys. This is the house you've took, and Hester here will look after you. I'll be goin'."

"No, you won't!" and Landon turned on him. "Why, man, we know nothing of this place. You stay till I dismiss you. I want a whole lot of information, but not till after we get lights and make the ladies comfortable."

"Comfortable! At Black Aspens! Not likely." The mocking laugh that accompanied these words struck terror to most of his hearers. "Nobody told me that you folks came up here to be comfortable."

"Shut up!" Landon's temper was near the breaking point. "Where's that woman with the lamps? Where's the man I engaged to look after things?"

"Hester, she's here. She'll be in in a minute. Thorpe, that's her husband, he's goin' to be a sort of butteler for you, he can't come till to morrow. But Hester, she's got supper ready, or will be, soon's you can wash up and all."

Hester came in then, a gaunt, hard featured New England woman, who looked utterly devoid of any emotion and most intelligence.

Stebbins, on the other hand, was apparently of keen perceptions and average intellect. His small blue eyes roved from one face to another, and though he looked sullen and disagreeable of disposition, he gave the effect of one ready to do his duty.

"All right," he said, as if without interest, "I'll set in the kitchen and wait. Hester here, she'll take the ladies to their rooms, and then after you get your supper, I'll tell you all you ask me. But I rented this place to you, I didn't agree to be a sign board and Farmers' Almanac."

"All right, old chap," and Landon smiled faintly, "but don't you get away till I see you. Now, girls, want to select your rooms?"

"Y—Yes," began Eve, bravely, and then a glance up the dark staircase made her shudder.

"What we want is light,—and plenty of it," broke in Braye. "Here you, Hester, I'll relieve you of that lamp you're holding, and you hop it, and get more,—six more,—twelve more—hear me?"

"We haven't that many in the house." Dull eyed the woman looked at him with that sublime stolidity only achieved by born New Englanders.

"Oh, you haven't! Well, bring all you have and to morrow you manage to raise a lot more. How many have you, all told?"

"Four, I think."

"Four! For a party of nine! Well, have you candles?"

"Half a dozen."

"And three candlesticks, I suppose! Bring them in, and if you're shy of candlesticks, bring old bottles,—or anything."

"Good for you, Braye, didn't know you had so much generalship," and Gifford Bruce clapped his nephew on the shoulder. "I'm glad I don't believe in ghosts, for every last one of you people are shaking in your shoes this minute! What's the matter with you? Nothing has happened."

"It was that awful ride through the woods," said Vernie, cuddling into her uncle's arm. "I—I like it,—I like it all,—but, the local colour is so—so dark!"

"That's it, Kiddie," said Braye, "the local colour is about the murkiest I ever struck. But here are our lights, hooray!"

Hester brought two more small hand lamps, and after another trip to the kitchen brought six candles and six battered but usable candlesticks.

A candle was given to each of the four women, and Norma politely selected the oldest and most broken holder.

"Land sake!" exclaimed Stebbins, coming in, "you goin' to use that candlstick? That's the very one the murderin' woman used!"

With a scream, Norma dropped it and no one moved to pick it up.

"Get out, Stebbins!" roared Landon, "you queer the whole business."

"I'll take this one," and Mr. Bruce picked up the old brass affair; "I'm not afraid of such things. Here, Miss Cameron, take mine, it's new and commonplace, I assure you."

White faced and trembling, Norma took the cheap crockery thing, and shortly they all followed Hester up the stairs to the shadows of the floor above. The place was silent as the grave. Hester's slippered feet made no sound, and a voluntary scraping of Tracy's shoes stopped as soon as he realized its enormous sound in those empty halls. A multitude of doors led to rooms in all directions, there seemed to be no plan or symmetry of any sort. The candle flames flickered, the small lamps burned with a pale sickly light.

Hester paused midway of the main corridor.

"What rooms you want?" she asked, uninterestedly.

"Give me a cheerful one," wailed Milly. "Oh, Wynne, let us take a little, cozy one."

"Of course you shall," said Braye, kindly. "Hester, which is the pleasantest room in the house? Give that to Mr. and Mrs. Landon! And then we'll put all you girls near them. The rest of us will camp anywhere."

"Let's all pretty much camp anywhere till tomorrow," suggested the Professor. "I'd like to select my room by daylight."

"I've made up some of the rooms, and some I ain't," volunteered Hester.

"Then, for Heaven's sake, show us the made up rooms, and get out!" burst forth Landon. "I wish we'd brought our maids, Milly; that woman affects me like fever and ague."

But after a time they were assigned to various more or less inhabitable bedrooms, and as quickly as possible, all reappeared in the great hall below, ready for supper.

The dining room, toward the back of the house, was not half bad, after all the available lights had been commandeered for the table.

"You knew there were no electrics," said Braye to Eve, who was bewailing the fact.

"Of course I did, and I thought candles would be lovely and picturesque and all that; and kerosene gives a good soft light, but—well, somehow,—do you know what I thought as we came through that dreadful wood?"

"What?"

"Only one sentence rang through my mind,—and that was,—The Powers of Darkness!"

"That isn't a sentence," objected the Professor, a little querulously, and everybody laughed. Also, everybody blessed the occasion for laughter.

But Eve went on. "I don't care if it's a sentence or a syllogism, or what it is! It just rang in my ears. And I tell you this whole place is under the Powers of Darkness—"

"Do hush, Eve," pleaded Milly. "I was just beginning to pull myself together, and now you've upset me again!"

"But Milly,—"

"Let up, Eve! For the love of Mike, let up! You're enough to give anybody the creeps." Landon glared at her.

"It's only a question of light," Tracy broke in, in his pleasant way. "Now, we've light enough for the moment, and to morrow we'll make this the house of a thousand candles and a hundred lamps, and a few lanterns if you like. Incidentally, Friend Hester makes first rate doughnuts."

"Aren't they bully!" chimed in Vernie. "I've eaten six, and here goes for another."

"Lucky they're small," said her uncle. "But seven doughnuts are enough to make you see the ghost of old Montgomery himself!"

"And all the Green Mountain boys," added Tracy, who was determined to keep conversation away from fearsome subjects.

By the time they had finished the meal, every one felt more at ease, Landon had recovered his poise, and Milly her cheerfulness.

"Now, then," the Professor asked, as they left the table, "shall we explore the house to night—"

"Lord, no!" cried Braye. "Leave it lay till daylight. Also, don't quiz old Stebbins as to who's who in Black Aspens! Let's turn on the Victrola and dance, or let's play poker or sing glees, or anything that's a proper parlour trick. But nothing, I insist, pertaining to our mission up here. That'll keep."

"As you like," and now Landon could smile. "And you mollycoddles may pursue those light minded pleasures. But I'm going to have it out with Steb, because I want to know some several Laws for Beginners. But, don't let me interfere with your plans. Go ahead, and have play 'Hide and Seek All Over the House,' if you choose. That used to be my favourite indoor game."

"Oh!" squealed Vernie, "what an awful suggestion! In this house!"

"I move we hear the story of the house to night. — right now," said Eve.

Milly clasped her hands over her ears, instead of, as usual, over her mouth, and cried, "No! I forbid it! Don't let 'em, will you, Wynne?"

"Seems to me," remarked Mr. Stebbins, "you folks don't know your own minds! You want a ha'nted house, then when you git it, you're too scared to hear the story of the ha'nt."

"I'm not scared," asserted Norma, "but somehow, a ha'nt sounds so much worse than a haunt. Doesn't it, now?"

"It sure does," agreed Braye. "A ha'nt is concrete, while a haunt is abstract."

"Good!" and Hardwick nodded approval. "Now, I suggest that we look around a bit, get the general lay of the house and then all go to bed early. A good night's sleep will put our nerves and muscles in condition again. I'm delighted with the place, and I foresee a first class vacation ahead of us."

"I wish it was behind us, and we were just starting for home," murmured Milly, but Eve reprimanded her.

"Don't be a spoilsport! I like the place too, Professor, and I'm going to investigate a little. What room is this?"

Eve's graceful figure crossed the great square hall, where they were all standing about, and paused at the closed door of a room just at the right hand as one entered the house.

"Why, it's locked!" she exclaimed. "That won't do, Mr. Stebbins! This whole domain is ours, now, you know. Open this door, please."

Eve wore the light gray skirt of her travelling costume, and a thin sheer white silk blouse, whose V'd neck fell away from her long, slender throat. Her hand on the door knob, she suddenly turned her strange beryl eyes toward Stebbins, her face turning whiter and her thin lips redder as she gazed.

"This is the room—isn't it?" she breathed, and her hand slowly fell from the knob and hung loosely at her side.

"Yes, ma'am," replied Stebbins, stolidly. "How'd you know?"

"How could I help knowing!" and Eve's voice rang out like a clarion. "I see it! I see it all!"

She rushed across the hall and fell trembling on a settee. Tracy flew to her side, and took her hand.

"There, there, Miss Carnforth, brace up! We're all right here. Nothing can hurt you."

"Beats all how she knew!" muttered Stebbins. "You see that's the room—"

A cry from Milly stirred Landon to action.

"Drop it, Stebbins," he said, and took a step toward him. "None of that to night. We do want your haunted house, but the long journey up here, and your confounded negligence in the matter of lights and servants and general good will, has got on the ladies' nerves. Beat it now, to the kitchen, or wherever your quarters are, but you stay here to night and be ready to report in the morning. You hear me?"

"Yes, sir," and shrugging his shoulders, the man disappeared among the shadows in the back of the hall.

The great main hall was so large that the lights they had were all insufficient for illumination. There seemed to be innumerable doors and openings of side corridors, also a second staircase, far behind the main one.

"Here's a good looking room, let's go in here," said Tracy, stepping through some old, faded draperies to the room on the left of the hall as one entered the house.

Hardwick followed, and the others with lamps and candles pushed in. It was a large, dignified apartment, evidently a parlour or ballroom of the old mansion. The furniture was of old, carved rosewood, its upholstery worn, but fairly decent. Oil portraits were on the walls and massive ornaments of imitation bronze stood about, showing white here and there where the coating was chipped off.

Yellowish onyx vases graced the mantels, and the windows were hung with heavy rep curtains which, however, veiled no lighter ones.

"Ghastly!" cried Norma.

"What do you mean by ghastly?" began the Professor, and Tracy laughed.

"She didn't mean it at all, Professor," he said, "Miss Cameron meant to say hideous. Now, don't ask me what I mean by hideous, just look at the interior decorations here and draw your own conclusions as to my meaning. But though not to be called aesthetic, this furniture is fairly comfy. The springs of this sofa are intact,—come sit by my side, little darling." This last to Vernie, who was wide eyed and alert, lapping up these strange, new impressions.

"All right," and she flung herself down beside him. "You're a real comfort, Mr. Tracy,—you're so,—so— unministerial!"

"Thank you, my child. One needn't carry one's pulpit voice into social life."

"Oh, I don't mean you do or say anything that a man of your calling oughtn't to, but you're so nice about it."

"I think so too," chattered Milly, "I do think a clergyman with a sense of humour makes a fine combination."

The mental atmosphere gradually lightened and when Landon suggested they all retire, it was a composed and merry hearted group that obeyed the summons.

When twelve sonorous strokes boomed from the tall clock in the upper hall, the men beneath the roof of Black Aspens were all sleeping more or less soundly.

Milly, with only occasional little quivering shudders, slumbered in Landon's arms. Vernie slept with the sound dreamless sleep of youth.

But Eve and Norma were wide awake, and unable to close their eyes.

In adjoining rooms, the communicating door ajar, they could hear one another toss restlessly, but they said no words.

Norma's blue eyes were wide open, her thoughts rambling over the strange surroundings in which she found herself, and her mind leaping forward, speculating on what might happen.

Eve, her long, glittering eyes half closed, listened for any sound; her nerves alert, her thoughts darting from material things to the supernatural, every muscle tense with a nameless apprehension.

More hours were rung out by the old clock, and at last dawn began to creep in at the deep narrow windows of the old house.

With a shrug and a stretch Vernie awoke. Drowsily, in the half light she tried to make out her surroundings, and then, suddenly remembering where she was, she dove her head under her blanket, in a quick rush of fear. Then curiosity conquered, and she came to the surface again, and looked about. The light, growing gradually stronger, showed the appointments of the room, the ugly old four poster bedstead, of light wood,—apple or hickory,—the heavy rep lambrequins, that seemed to be a feature of the house, and the scantily appointed dresser, on which, the night before, she had set her extinguished candle.

Shadows still lurked in the corners of the room, still hung round the draperies and furniture, yet through the gloom Vernie saw something that made her eyes stare and her flesh creep. Clenching her hands till her sharp nails bit into her palms, she gave a shriek that rang through the silent house.

CHAPTER 4: THE STORY OF THE HOUSE

FROM their nearby rooms Eve and Norma rushed to Vernie's room.

The child was huddled beneath the bed clothes and at their entrance shot her head out, crying wildly, "Look! look! the old candlestick!" Milly came running, in dressing gown and slippers, and from distant regions came the voices of the men.

"What's the matter?" asked Gifford Bruce.

"Wasn't that Vernie's voice?"

"Yes, Uncle Gif," Vernie called out. "Oh, did you do it?"

"Do what?" and in his hastily donned bath robe, old Mr. Bruce appeared.

"Why," and Vernie was calm now, "there's that old candlestick, the one the—the murderer used—on my dresser! Last night I had a little china one!"

"What are you talking about—a murderer! Wake up, child!"

"I'm not asleep. But I see, now. You had this old one, Uncle Gif, and, you know you said you were going to fool us if you could, and so you sneaked it in here to pretend the haunt did it!"

"What! What nonsense! I did nothing of the sort!"

"Who did, then? You know you had this one last night."

"I certainly did. Wonder what's in my room now."

Mr. Bruce ran back to his room and returned with the little china candlestick Vernie had carried to her room the night before. They had certainly been exchanged during the night.

Everybody stared at the two candles, so worthless in themselves, but so inexplicably transferred, if, as he declared, Gifford Bruce had not exchanged them.

"Of course I didn't do it," he repeated, angrily. "I did say, in fun, that I meant to trick you, but when I saw how nervous and wrought up all you women were last night, I wouldn't dream of doing such a thing! Why, Vernie, I think too much of you, dear, to add to your fear or discomfort in any way."

At last everybody concluded it was the work of some one of their number, and there were varying opinions as to the identity of the perpetrator of what must have been meant for a joke.

But at breakfast time the matter was discussed very seriously and each avowed in all honour that he or she knew nothing of it.

"I can speak not only for myself," said Professor Hardwick, gravely, "but for Mr. Tracy and Mr. Braye. They would have had to pass my door to move around the halls, and I was awake all night, looking and listening, and I know they did not leave their rooms."

"I speak for myself," said Gifford Bruce, haughtily. "I declare on my oath that I did not leave my bed. Somebody exchanged those candles,—but it was not I."

The Landons spoke for each other, and no one, of course, could suspect Wynne or Milly. And naturally, the two girls, Eve and Norma, would not go to Mr. Bruce's room to play a trick like that.

"I don't mind now," said Vernie, "when it's all light and cheerful and you're all around me, and the breakfast is so good and all. I think it's the beginning of these experiences we came up here to look for. Why are you all so surprised? Because *I* had the first party?"

The merry eyed girl was unafraid now, but Hardwick shook his head.

"I don't like it," he said. "We can't investigate if there's a trickster among us. You didn't do it yourself, did you, Vernie?"

"No, Professor," and the pure truthful gaze of the brown eyes left no room for disbelief. "Honest, I didn't. But," she laughed mischievously, "if I had, I should *say* I hadn't!"

"Vernie! This won't do!" and Eve glared at her, "You little minx, I believe you did do it!"

"Don't you look at me like that, Eve Carnforth! Stop it! You scare me." Vernie fairly cowered before Eve's basilisk eyes. "I believe you did it!"

"There, there, girls," broke in Tracy, with his gentle smile, "don't get to hair pulling. If we've all finished breakfast, let's now hear the story of the house, and then we can tell if its patron ghost is the sort given to exchanging bedroom furniture o' nights."

"Yes," agreed Norma, "I'm crazy to hear the story. Where's Mr. Stebbins, does anybody know?"

"I'll dig him up," Landon assured them. "Where shall we congregate?"

"In the drawing room," said Milly, "that's the only room I'm not afraid of."

"I'm fearfully afraid of that!" said Tracy, in mock terror. "Those rep lambrequins get on my nerves!"

"Aren't they awful!" and Norma laughed. "They don't frighten me, but they jar my aesthetics terribly."

"No," said Elijah Stebbins, firmly, as the conclave began, "not in that there parlour. Here in the hall. You folks want this house, you want the story of this house, now you sit here to hear it."

"Very well," said Braye, agreeably. "Just as you say, Mr. Stebbins. Now begin at the beginning, but don't drool too long a spiel."

The whole party grouped themselves in the great hall, and for the first time began to take in the details of its appointments. Though in disrepair as to walls and cornices, the lines of its architecture were fine and it was of noble proportions; the staircase was beautifully planned; and the wonderful bronze doors, which they had not examined the night before, were truly works of art.

"The old Montgomery who brought them doors from Italy, pretty much built the house behind 'em," Stebbins volunteered, "and them colyums, of course, come with the doors. They're some valu'ble, I'm told. You see, the doors is the same outside and in, and the colyums is, too. Well, then, he had the vestibule of murhoggany, to sort o' set off the bronze, I s'pose, and the rest of the walls is marble,— solid old Vermont marble, which Lord knows was to be had for the pickin', up here."

"Get along to the story, Steb," urged Landon.

"Yes, sir. Well, the Montgomery that built this house,—though, it was part built before, he added on to his father's house,—well, he was a daredevil, and a tyrant. Little mite of a man, but full of the old Nick. And, as those little men will do, he married a reg'lar Hessian of a woman. Big, sort o' long and gaunt, they say she was, and a termagant for sure! She led him a life, and also, he led her one. For he was a terror and so was she. What he lacked in size he made up in temper, and she had both. Well, here's the story.

"He took sick, and she nursed him. They didn't have trained nurses and specialists in them days. Now some says, he was jest naturally took sick and some says, that she give him slow poison. But, be that as it may, one night, she give him prussic acid, and he died. She threw a shawl over her head, and ran screamin' to the village for the doctor. I s'pose remorse got her, for she confessed, and said 'I killed him! I killed him! At four o'clock I killed him!'

"She went crazy, they say, then and there. Well, the doctor he said he'd come right away, but she ran home first. And he followed 's fast 's he could, and—when he come, here was the woman,—and she was a washin' the dead man's lips,—she said, to get the smell of the bitter ammonds off,—you know, prussic acid is for all the world the smell of bitter almonds. The doctor, he found the man was really dead, and he was for havin' her arrested, but she was so plumb crazy, he decided to take her to an asylum instead.

"He had to go off to get help, and he left her,—here alone in this house with the body. They was in that room," Stebbins pointed to the room with the locked door, at the right hand of the hall as one entered, "the room with the tassels, it's called."

"Why is it called that?" broke in Eve, whose piercing eyes were fairly glittering with excitement, "what sort of tassels?"

"Great heavy tassels on the curtains and lambaquins, ma'am,—want to see it?"

"Not now," ordained Landon, "the story first."

"Well," resumed Stebbins, "they was in that room, the dead husband and the live wife, when the doctor went away, and because he knew she was out of her head, he locked 'em in. And when he came back—she was setting there, just where he'd left her, still in a dazed sort o' stupor, and—the corpse was gone."

"Gone! where?" rasped out the Professor.

"Nobody knows. Nobody ever knew. It had just disappeared from off the face of the earth. The doctor and the village folks all agreed that it was sperrited away. 'Cause that woman,—she couldn't get out o' the doors to cart it off, and she couldn't 'a' got out of a winder with it, without showin' some signs, and if she had, what in the world could she 'a' done with it? It wasn't buried nowhere around, and if she'd 'a' threw it in the lake, s'posin' she'd got out a winder, how'd she got in again? Anyhow, that's the story, and they all said she was a witch and she bewitched the body away, so's the doctor and sheriff couldn't smell the prussic acid on it and hang her for murder. They searched and searched but they couldn't find no signs of her havin' even moved outen her chair. She sat there like a dead woman herself, when the doctor left her and likewise when he come back."

"The tale is very circumstantial," observed Gifford Bruce, a bit drily.

"I'm tellin' it as I've many a time heard it, sir," said Stebbins, a little resentfully. "This here story's been common talk around these parts a many years, and I ain't one to add to nor take from it."

"Go on," commanded Landon, briefly.

"They put her away, in a loonytic asylum, and she died in it. They never found hide nor hair of the dead man, and the place fell to some kin that lived down Pennsylvania way. They come up here for a while, I b'lieve, but the ha'nt scared 'em off. It's been sold some several times and at last it fell to my father's family. Now it's mine, and it's a white elephant to me. I can't sell or rent it, and so you folks may well believe I jumped at the chance to have you take it for a spell."

"We haven't heard about the haunt yet," said Norma. She spoke quietly, but her lips quivered a little, and her fingers were nervously picking at her handkerchief.

"That," and Stebbins looked even more sombre than he had, "that's my own experience, so I can give it to you first hand.

"I come here to live, 'bout ten years ago, and I was plucky enough to hoot at ghost stories and tales o' ha'nts.

"So I set out to sleep in that—that room with the tassels,—out o' sheer bravado. But I got enough of it."

The man's head fell on his breast and he paused in his narrative.

"Go on," said Landon, less brusquely than before.

Milly stirred nervously. "Don't let him tell the rest, Wynne," she said.

"Oh, yes, dear. Remember, this is what we're here for."

Most of the men shifted their positions; Hardwick leaned forward, both hands on his knees. Gifford Bruce sat with one arm flung carelessly over his chair back, a slight smile on his face.

Braye was beside Norma, and watched alternately her face and Eve's, while Tracy was holding Vernie's hand, and his gentle calm kept the volatile child quiet.

"I see it all so plainly,—that first night—" Stebbins said, slowly. "*First* night! Land! there never was another! Not for me. I'd sooner 'a' died than slep' in that room again!"

"See a ghost?" asked Bruce, flippantly.

"Yes, sir," and Stebbins looked straight at him. "I seen a ghost. I'm a sound sleeper, I am, and I went to sleep quiet and ca'm as a baby. I woke as the big clock there was a strikin' four. It was that what woke me—I hope."

"Is there—is there a bed in that room?" asked the Professor.

"Lord, yes, it was them folkses bedroom. In them days, people most always slep' downstairs. I come awake suddenly, and the room was full of an icy chill. Not just coldness, but a damp chill—like undertakers' iceboxes."

Vernie shuddered and Tracy held her hand more firmly. Landon slipped his arm round Milly, and Eve and Norma glanced at each other.

Gifford Bruce replaced his sneering smile, which had somehow disappeared.

"It was winter, and plumb dark at four o'clock in the morning, but the room was full of an unearthly light,—a sort of frosty, white glow, like you see in a graveyard sometimes.

"And comin' toward me was a tall, gaunt figure, with a shawl over its head, a white, misty shape, that had a sort of a halting step but was comin' straight and sure toward that bed I was lyin' on. I tried to scream, I tried to move, but I couldn't,—I was paralyzed. On and on came the thing—halting at every step, but gettin' nearer and nearer. As she—oh, I knew it was that woman—"

"I thought it was a man who was murdered," put in Mr. Bruce, in his most sardonic tones.

"So it was, sir," Stebbins spoke mildly, "but it was the murderess doin' the ha'ntin'. I s'pose she can't rest quiet in her grave for remorse and that. She came nearer and—and I saw her face—and—"

"Well?"

"And it was a skull! A grinning skull. And her long bony hand held a glass—a glass of poison—for me."

"Er—did you take it?" This from Bruce.

"No, sir. I swooned away, or whatever you may call it. I lost all consciousness, and when I come to, the thing was gone."

"Ever see her again?" inquired Mr. Bruce, conversationally.

"No, sir," and Stebbins eyed him uninterestedly. It was impossible to annoy the story teller. "No, I never *seen* her."

"Heard her?" asked Braye.

"Yes; many's the time. But—I ain't never slept in that room since."

"I should say not!" cried Eve. "But I will! I'll brave the phantasm. I'd be glad to see her. I'm not afraid."

"You needn't be," said Mr. Bruce, with a short laugh. "You won't see anything, Miss Carnforth. I'd be willing to try it, too."

"What other manifestations have you experienced?" asked Braye. "What have you heard?"

"Mostly groans–"

"And hollow laughter," interrupted Bruce. "Those are the regulation sounds, I believe."

"Oh, hush!" cried Eve. "Mr. Bruce, you drive me frantic! I wish you hadn't come!"

"I don't," declared Bruce. "I think it's most interesting. And do I understand, Mr. Stebbins, that this charming lady of large size and hard heart, carried usually that candlestick that I made use of last night?"

At last Stebbins resented Bruce's chaff.

"So the story goes, sir," he said, curtly. "And many's the time I've known that candlestick to be moved during the night, by no mortal hand."

"Look here, Uncle Gif," said Braye, good-naturedly, "you don't want to get yourself disliked, do you? Now, let up on your quizzing, and let's get down to business. We set out for a haunted house. I, for one, think we've got all we came after, and then some! If the ha'nt began moving her candlestick around the first night, what may she not do next? You didn't do it, did you, Uncle?"

"I've told you I didn't, Rudolph, and I again repeat my word. But it was scarcely necessary for me to do it, when such a capable spook,—I mean, phantasm is regularly in attendance."

"Now, I've told you the tale," and Stebbins rose, and shook himself as if he had done his duty. "I ain't nowise responsible for your believin' it. What I've told you is true, so far's my own experience goes; and what I've told you hearsay, is the old story that's been told up in these parts by one generation after another, since old Montgomery's day. Now do you want to see the room with the tassels?"

"I don't!" cried Milly, "I can't stand any more."

"You needn't, dear," said Landon; "suppose you go out on the terrace and walk about in the sunlight. You go with her, Vernie, you can see the room, later on."

"I'll go too," and Tracy tactfully offered his escort. "The tassels will keep. Come on, Braye?"

"No; I'll see the show through. You can look after the ladies, Tracy."

So the others crowded round Stebbins, as he prepared to unlock the door of the fatal room.

"Tain't no great sight," he said, almost apologetically. "But it's the ha'nted room."

Slowly he turned the key and they all filed in.

The room was dark, save for what light came in from the hall. All blinds were closed, and over the windows hung heavy curtains of rep that had once been red but was now a dull, nondescript colour. There were more of these heavy, long curtains, evidently concealing alcoves or cupboards, and over each curtain was a "lambrequin" edged with thick twisted woolen fringe, and at intervals, tassels,—enormous, weighty tassels, such as were once used in church pulpits and other old fashioned upholstery. Such quantities of these there were, that it is small wonder the room received its name.

And the tassels had a sinister air. Motionless they hung, dingy, faded, but still of an individuality that seemed to say, "we have seen unholy deed,— we cry out mutely for vengeance!"

"It was them tassels that scared me most," Stebbins said, in an awed tone. "I mean before—she come. They sort of swayed,—when they wasn't no draught nor anything."

"I don't wonder!" said Braye, "they're the ghostliest things I ever saw! But the whole room is awful! It—oh I say! put up a window!"

"I can't," said Stebbins simply. "These here windows ain't been up for years and years. The springs is all rusted and won't work."

"There's something in the room!" cried Eve, hysterically, "I mean—something—besides us—something alive!"

"No, ma'am," said Stebbins, solemnly, "what's in here ain't alive, ma'am. I ain't been in here myself, since that night I slep' here, and I wouldn't be now, only to show you folks the room. I sort of feel 's if I'd shifted the responsibility to you folks now. I don't seem to feel the same fear of the ha'nt, like I was here alone."

"*Don't* say ha'nt! Stop it!" and Eve almost shrieked at him.

"Yes, ma'am. Ghost, ma'am. But ha'nt it is, and ha'nt it will be, till the crack o' doom. Air ye all satisfied with your bargain?"

No one answered, for every one was conscious of a subtle presence and each glanced fearfully, furtively about, nerves shaken, wills enfeebled, vitality low.

"What is it?" whispered Eve.

"Imagination!" declared Mr. Bruce, but he shook his shoulders as he spoke, as if ridding himself of an incubus.

There was a chilliness that was not like honest cold, there was a stillness that was not an ordinary silence, and there was an impelling desire in every heart to get out of that room and never return.

But all were game, and when at last Stebbins said, "Seen enough?" they almost tumbled over one another in a burst of relief at the thought of exit. The great hall seemed cheerful by contrast, and Landon, in a voice he strove to make matter of fact, said, "Thank you, Stebbins, you have certainly given us what we asked for."

"Yes, sir. Did you notice it, sir?"

"What?"

"The smell—the odour—in that room?"

"I did," said Eve, "I noticed the odour of prussic acid."

"Yes, ma'am," said Stebbins, "that's what I meant."

CHAPTER 5: EVE'S EXPERIENCE

THE investigators had investigated for a week. They were now having tea in the great hall, to whose shadowy distances and shabby appointments they had become somewhat accustomed.

Kept up to the mark by the Landons, old Jed Thorpe had developed positive talents as a butler, and with plenty of lamps and candles, and a couple of willing, if ignorant maids, the household machinery ran fairly smoothly. Supplies were procured in East Dryden or sent up from New York markets and by day the party was usually a gay hearted, merry mannered country house group.

Every day at tea time, they recounted any individual experiences that might seem mysterious, and discussed them.

"It's this way," Professor Hardwick summed up; "the determining factor is the dark. Ghosts and haunted houses are all very well at night, but daylight dispels them as a sound breaks silence."

"What about my experience when I slept in the Room with the Tassels," growled Gifford Bruce.

Braye laughed. "You queered yourself, Uncle Gif, when you announced before we started, that you were not bound to good faith. Your ghost stories are discounted before you tell 'em!"

"But I did see a shape,—a shadowy form, like a tall woman with a shawl over her head—"

"You dreamed it," said Milly, smiling at him.

"Or else—"

"Milly daren't say it," laughed Eve, "but I will. Or else, you invented the yarn."

"If I'm to be called a—"

"Tut, tut, Mr. Bruce," intervened Tracy, "nobody called you one! Playful prevarication is all right, especially as you warned us you'd fool us if you could. Now I can tell an experience and justly expect to be believed."

"But you haven't had any," and Eve's translucent eyes turned to him.

"I have," began Tracy, slowly, "but they've been a bit indefinite. It's unsatisfactory to present only an impression or a suggestion, where facts are wanted. And the Professor says truly that hints and haunts are convincing at night, but repeated, at a pleasant, comfortable tea hour, they sound flimsy and unconvincing."

"What did you think you saw or heard?" asked Norma, with a reminiscent, far off look in her eyes.

"Every morning, or almost every morning, at four o'clock, I seem to hear the trailing robes of a presence of some sort. I seem to hear a faint moaning sound, that is like nothing human."

"That's imagination," said Braye, promptly.

"It is, doubtless," agreed Hardwick, "but it is due to what may be called 'expectant attention.' If we had not connected four o'clock with the story of this house, Mr. Tracy would not have those hallucinations at that time."

"Perhaps so," the clergyman looked thoughtful. "But it seems vivid and real at the time. Then, in the later morning, it is merely a hazy memory."

"You know Mr. Stebbins said that every one who died in this house always died at four o'clock."

"I know he said so," and Braye looked quizzical.

"Oh, come now, don't doubt honest old Stebbins!" and Eve frowned. "We must believe his tales or we'll never get anywhere. I'm going over to East Dryden to see him to morrow, I want a few more details; And, it seems to me, we're getting nowhere,—with our imaginations and hallucinations. Now, to night, I'm going to sleep in the

Room with the Tassels. I've no fear of it, and I have a deep and great curiosity."

"Oh, let me sleep there with you! Mayn't I, Eve? Oh, please let me!" Vernie danced about in her eagnerness, and knelt before Eve, pleading.

"No, Vernie, I forbid it," said her uncle, decidedly. "If Miss Carnforth wants to do this thing, I have nothing to say, but you must not, my child. I know you people don't believe me, but I surely saw an apparition the night I slept there, and it was no human trickster. Neither was it hallucination. I was as wideawake as I am now—"

"We know the rest, Uncle Gif," and Braye laughingly interrupted the recital. "Stalking ghost, hollow groans, and—were there clanking chains?"

"There were not, but in its shrouded hand the spectre held a glass—"

"Of prussic acid, of which you smelt the strong odour! Yes, I know,—but it won't go down, old chap "

"The prussic acid won't?" and Landon chuckled.

"Nor the tale either," said the Professor. "It's too true. The shawled woman filled the specifications too accurately to seem convincing."

"You're a nice crowd," grumbled Mr. Bruce. "Come up here for experiences and then hoot at the first real thing that happens."

"All your own fault," retorted Norma. "If you hadn't advertised your propensity for fooling us, your word would have carried weight."

"All right, let somebody else sleep in that room, then. But not Miss Carnforth. Let one of the men try it."

"Thank you, none for me," said Braye. "I detest shawled women waking me up at four o'clock, to take my poison!"

"I'll beg off, too," said Tracy. "I wake at four every morning anyway, with those aspen boughs shivering against my windows. I'd trim them off, but that doesn't seem like playing the game."

"Wynne shan't sleep there, and that settles *that*," and Milly's grasp on her husband's coat sleeve was evidently sufficiently detaining.

"That leaves only me, of the men," asserted the Professor. "I'm quite willing to sleep in that room. Indeed, I want to. I've only been waiting till I felt sure of the house, the servants and—excuse me, the members of our own party! Now, I've discovered that the servants' quarters can be securely locked off, so that they cannot get in this part of the house; I've found that the outside doors and the windows can be fastened against all possibility of outside intrusion; and, I shall stipulate that our party shall so congregate in a few rooms, that no one can—ahem,—haunt my slumbers without some one else knowing it. I'll ask you three young ladies to sleep in one room and allow me to lock you in. Or two adjoining rooms, to which I may hold all keys. Mr. Tracy, Mr. Bruce and Mr. Braye, I shall arrange similarly, while the Landons must also consent to be imprisoned by me. This is the only way I can make a fair test. Will you all agree?"

"Splendid!" cried Eve, "of course we will. But, Professor, let me try it first. If you should have a weird experience, it might scare me off, but now I am brave enough. Oh, please, do that! Let me lock you all in your rooms, and let me sleep in the Room with the Tassels to night! Oh, please say yes, all of you! I must, I *must* try it!" The girl looked like a seeress, as, with glittering eyes and flushed cheeks she plead her cause.

"Why, of course, if you want to, Miss Carnforth," said the Professor, looking at her admiringly. "I'll be glad to have the benefit of your experience before testing myself. And there is positively no danger. As I've said, the locks, bolts, and bars are absolutely safe against outside intrusion, or visits from the servants. Though we know they are not to be suspected. And as you are not afraid of the supernatural, I can see no argument against your plan."

"Suppose I go with you," suggested Norma, her large blue eyes questioning Eve Carnforth's excited face.

"No, Norma, not this time. I prefer to be alone. I'll lock you and Vernie in your room; I'll lock Milly and Wynne in their room; I'll lock you four men in two rooms, and then, I'll know—I'll know that whatever I see or hear is not a fraud or trick of anybody. And I think you can trust me to tell you the truth in the morning."

"If there's anything to tell," supplemented Braye. "I think, Eve, as to ghosts, you're cutting off your source of supply."

"Then we'll merely prove nothing. But I'm determined to try."

Again Vernie begged to be allowed to share Eve's experiences, but neither Mr. Bruce, nor Eve herself would consider the child's request.

"Every one of us," the Professor said, musingly, "has told of hearing mysterious sounds and of seeing mysterious shadows, but,—except for Bruce's graphic details!—all our observations have been vague and uncertain. They may well have been merely imagination. But Miss Carnforth is not imaginative, I mean, not so, to the exclusion of a fair judgment of what her senses experience. Therefore I shall feel, if she sees nothing to night, that I shall see nothing when I sleep in that room to morrow night."

"I am especially well adapted for the test," Eve said, though in no way proudly, "for I have a premonition that the phantasm will appear to me more readily than to some others. Remember, I knew that was the haunted room before we had been told. I knew it before we entered the house that first night. It was revealed to me, as other things have been even during our stay here. You must realize that I am a sensitive, and so better fitted for these visitations than a more phlegmatic or practical person."

"What else has been revealed to you, Eve?" asked Braye.

"Perhaps revealed isn't just the word, Rudolph, but I've seen more than most of you, I've heard voices, rustling as of wings, and other inexplicable sounds, that I know were audible only to me."

"Lord, Eve, you give me the creeps! Finished your tea? Come out for a walk then. Let's get off these subjects, if only for half an hour."

That night, Eve Carnforth carried out her plans to the letter.

Gifford Bruce, and his nephew Braye in one room; the Professor and Tracy in another, were locked in by Eve, amid much gaiety of ceremony.

"Set a thief to catch a thief," Braye declared. "Tracy, look after the Professor, that he doesn't jump out of the window, and you, Professor, watch Tracy!"

"They can't jump out the windows," said Eve, practically, "they're too high. And if they could, they couldn't get in the tasseled room. Those windows won't open. And, too, I know the Professor won't let Mr. Tracy out of his sight, or *vice versa*. Rudolph, you tie your uncle, if he shows signs of roving."

Eve's strong nerves gave no sign of tension as she completed all her precautionary arrangements. She locked the doors that shut off the servants' quarters; she locked the Landons in their room, she locked the door of the room that Norma and Vernie occupied, and at last, with various gay messages shouted at her through the closed portals, she went downstairs to keep her lonely vigil.

She did not undress, for she had no intention of sleeping that night. A kimono, and her hair comfortably in a long braid were her only concessions to relaxation.

She lay down on the hard old bed, and gazed about her. A single lamp lit the room, and she had a candle also, in case she desired to use it.

The light made strange shadows, the heavy, faded hangings seemed to sway and move, but whether they really did so or not, Eve couldn't determine. She got up and went to examine them. The feel of them was damp and unpleasant, they seemed to squirm under her hand, and she hastily dropped them and returned to the bed.

There was an uncanny, creepy atmosphere that disturbed her, in spite of her strong nerves and indomitable will.

She had locked the door, now she arose and took the key out and laid it on a table. She had heard that a key in a lock could be turned from the other side.

Then, on a sudden impulse, she put out the lamp, feeling utter darkness preferable to those weird shadows. But the darkness was too horrible, so she lighted the candle. It was not in the historic old brass candlestick, but in a gay affair of red china, and the homely, cheap thing somewhat reassured her, as a bit of modernity and real life.

She listened for a long time, imagining sighs or sounds, which she could not be sure she really heard. The whispering aspens outside were audible, and their continued soughing was monotonously annoying, but not frightful, because she had accustomed herself to it.

At last, her over wrought nerves wearied, her physical nature refused further strain, and Eve slept. A light, fitful sleep, interspersed with waking moments and with sudden swift dreams. But she kept fast hold of her perceptive faculties. If she slept and woke, she knew it. She heard the aspens' sounds, the hours struck by the great hall clock, and the sound of her own quick, short breathing.

Nothing else.

Until, just as the clock tolled the last stroke of four, she heard a low grating sound. Was some one at the door? She was glad she had taken out the key.

The candle still burned, but its tiny light rather accentuated than lifted the gloom of the shadowy room.

Slowly and noiselessly the door swung open, inward, into the room. Eve tried to sit up in bed, but could not.

She felt paralyzed, not so much frightened, as numbed with physical dread.

And then, with a slow gliding motion, *something* entered,—something tall, gaunt and robed in long, pale coloured draperies. It was unreal, shadowy in its aspect, it was only dimly visible in the gloom, but it gave the impression of a frightened, furtive personality that hesitated to move, yet was impelled to. A soft moan, as of despair, came from the figure, and it put out a long white hand and pinched out the candle flame. Then, with another sigh, Eve could *feel*, in the utter black darkness that the thing was coming to her side.

With all her might she tried to cry out, but her vocal cords were dumb, she made no sound. But she felt,—with all her senses, she *felt* the apparition draw nearer. At her bedside it paused, she knew this, by a sort of sixth sense, for she heard or saw nothing.

Then, she was conscious of a faint odour of prussic acid, its pungent bitterness unmistakable, though slight.

And then, a tiny flame, as of a wick without a candle, flashed for a second, disappeared, and Eve almost fainted. She did not entirely lose consciousness, but her brain reeled, her head seemed to spin round and her ears rang with a strange buzzing, for in the instant's gleam of that weird light, she had seen the face of the phantom, and—it was the face of a skull! It was the ghastly countenance of a death's head!

Half conscious, but listening with abnormal sense, she thought she descried the closing of the door, but could hear no key turn.

The knowledge that she was alone, gave her new life. She sprang up, lighted the candle, lighted the lamp, and looked about. All was as she had arranged it. The door was locked, the key, untouched, upon the table. Nothing was disturbed, but Eve Carnforth knew that her experience, whatever its explanation, had not been a dream.

When her senses had reeled, she had not lost entire control of them through her physical fear, she had kept her mental balance, and she knew that what her brain had registered had actually occurred.

Alert, she lay for a long time thinking it over. She felt sure there would be no return of the spectre,—she felt sure it had been a spectre,—and she was conscious of a feeling of curiosity rather than fright.

At last she rose, and unlocking the door, went out into the great hall. By the light of her lamp, she looked it over. The carved bronze doors between the enormous bronze columns, were so elaborately locked and bolted as to give almost the effect of a fortress.

The windows were fastened and some were barred. But all these details had been looked after in advance; Eve gazed at them now, in an idle quest for some hint of hitherto unsuspected ingress.

But there was none, and now the clock was striking five.

She went slowly upstairs, unlocked the various doors, without opening them, and then went to her own bedroom.

"What about it?" cried Norma, eagerly, running to Eve's room.

"A big story;" Eve returned, wearily. "But I'll tell it to you all at once. I'm going to get some sleep. Wake me at eight, will you, Norma?"

Disappointed, but helpless, as Eve closed her door upon the would be visitor, Norma went back and told Milly, who was waiting and listening.

"I don't like it," Norma said, "for by eight o'clock she can cook up a story to scare us all! I think two ought to sleep in that room at once."

"Go to bed," said Milly, sleepily. "And don't you suspect Eve Carnforth of making up a yarn or even dressing up the truth! She isn't that sort."

As to Eve's veracity, opinions were divided.

She told the whole story, directly after breakfast, to the whole group, the servants being well out of earshot. .

She told it simply and straightforwardly, just as it had happened to her. Her sincerity and accurate statements stood a fire of questions, a volley of sarcastic comments and a few assertions of unbelief.

Professor Hardwick believed implicitly all she said, and encouraged her to dilate upon her experiences. But in nowise did she add to them, she merely repeated or emphasized the various points without deviation from her first narrative.

Norma and Braye went for a walk, and frankly discussed it.

"Of course, Eve colours it without meaning to," declared Braye; "it couldn't have happened, you know. We were all locked in, and Lord knows none of us could have put that stunt over even if we had wanted to."

"Of course not; that locking in business was unnecessary, but it does prove that no human agency was at work. That leaves only Eve's imagination—or—the real thing."

"It wasn't the real thing," and Braye shook his head. "There ain't no such animal! But Eve's imagination is—"

"No. Mr. Braye, you're on the wrong tack. Eve's imagination is not the sort that conjures up phantoms. Vernie's might do that, or Mrs. Landon's,—but not Miss Carnforth's. She is psychic,—I know, because I am myself—"

"Miss Cameron,—Norma," and Braye became suddenly insistent, "don't you sleep in that infernal room, will you? Promise me you won't."

"Why?" and the big blue eyes looked at him in surprise. "As Sentimental Tommy used to say, 'I would fell like to!' Why shouldn't I?"

"Oh, I don't want you to," and Braye looked really distressed. "Promise me you won't—please."

"Why do you care? 'Fraid I'll be carried off by the Shawled Woman?"

"Ugh!" and Braye shivered. "I can't bear to think of you alone down there. I beg of you not to do it."

"But that's what we came for. We're to investigate, you know."

"Well, then promise you won't try it until after I do."

"Trickster! And if you never try it, I can't!"

"You see through me too well. But, at least, promise this. If you try it, don't go alone. Say, you and Miss Carnforth go together—"

"Hello, people," and Vernie ran round a corner, followed more slowly by Tracy. "We've had a great little old climb! Hundreds of thousands of feet up the mounting side,—wasn't it, Mr. Tracy?"

"Thar or tharabouts," agreed Tracy, smiling at the pretty child.

"And Mr. Tracy is the delightfullest man! He told me all the names of the wild flowers,—weeds, rather,—there weren't any flowers. And oh, *isn't* it exciting about Eve's ghost! I'm going to ballyrag Uncle Gif till he lets me sleep in that room. He'll *have* to give in at last!"

"Don't, Vernie," begged Braye. "What possesses all you girls! I wish we'd never started this racket! But you mustn't do it, Kiddie, unless, that is, you go with somebody else. But not alone."

"Why, Cousin Rudolph, what are you afraid of? Are you a mollycoddle?"

"No, child, I'm afraid for you. A shock like that, even an imaginary fright, might upset your reason and—"

"Fiddle de dee! my reason is deeper rooted than that! Come on, Mr. Tracy, I'll race you to that big hemlock tree!"

The two started off, Vernie's flying legs gaining ground at first, over Tracy's steady well trained running step.

Chapter 6: At Four o'Clock

THE game grew more absorbing. Most of the party managed to store up enough courage by day to last well into the darker and more mysterious hours. It was at four in the morning that manifestations were oftenest noticed. At that hour vague moanings and rustlings were reported by one or another of the interested investigators, but no human agency was found to account for these.

Many plans were tried for discovering the secret of the Room with the Tassels, but all scrutiny failed to show any secret panel or concealed entrance. Indeed, their measurings and soundings proved there could not possibly be any entrance to that room save the door from the hall.

Eve and Norma believed thoroughly in the actual haunt of the woman who had poisoned her husband. They had no difficulty in swallowing whole all the strange noises or sights and attributing them to supernatural causes.

Not so Gifford Bruce. He still held that it was all trickery, cleverly done by some of the party, but as this was so clearly impossible, his opinion carried no weight.

Professor Hardwick was open minded, but exceedingly alert of observation and ready to suspect anybody who would give him the slightest reason to do so. Nobody did, however, and the weird sounds continued at intervals. The other men were non committal, saying they hadn't yet sufficient data to base conclusions on.

Milly was nervous and hysterical, but controlled her feelings at Landon's plea, and awaited developments with the rest. Vernie was merely an excited child, gay with youthful spirits and ready to believe or disbelieve whatever the others did.

Soon after Eve's experience, which no one, unless Gifford Bruce, doubted, Professor Hardwick slept in the haunted room. He had no results of interest to report. He said he had lain awake for a few hours and then fell asleep not to waken until daylight. If the Shawled Woman prowled about, he did not see or hear her. This was disappointing, but Tracy tried with little better success. In the morning, after a wakeful but uneventful night, the clergyman found the old battered brass candlestick in the room.

It had not been there the night before, and he had locked the door as the others had done. This was inexplicable, but of slight interest compared to a real haunting.

"You might have made up a ghost story," Braye reproached him, "as Uncle Gifford did, and as Miss Carnforth—didn't!"

The last word was distinctly teasing and Eve frowned gaily at him, but did not defend herself. She knew her experience had occurred just as she had told it, and, deeply mystified, she was earnestly and eagerly awaiting more light.

One day Braye found it necessary to go down to New York for a couple of days on some business matters. Before leaving, he made Vernie promise she would not sleep alone in the haunted room while he was gone.

"I forbid it, child," he said. "Uncle Gif is so easy going that I've no doubt you could wheedle permission out of him, but I beg of you not to. You're too young to risk a nerve shock of that sort. If you want to try it with Miss Carnforth or Miss Cameron, all right, but not alone. Promise me, Flapper, and I'll bring you a pretty present from town day after to morrow."

Vernie laughingly gave the required promise, but it did not weigh heavily on her conscience, for no sooner had Braye really gone, than she confided to Mr. Tracy her indecision regarding the keeping of her word.

"Of course you'll keep your promise," and Tracy regarded her seriously. "Nice people consider a spoken word inviolable. I know you, Vernie; you like to talk at random, but I think you've an honourable nature."

So Vernie said nothing more to him, but she confided in Eve Carnforth her intention of sleeping in the Tasseled Room that very night.

Eve did not discourage her, and promised to tell no one.

The plan was easily carried out. As it was understood no one was sleeping in the haunted room, no special precautions were taken, save the usual locking up against outside intruders. And after the great locks and bolts were fastened on doors and windows, it would have been a clever burglar indeed who could have effected an entrance to Black Aspens.

The evening had been pleasantly spent. Some trials of the Ouija board, a favourite diversion, had produced no interesting results, and rather early they all retired.

At midnight, Vernie softly rose, and went downstairs alone in the darkness. A night lamp in the upper hall gave a faint glimmer below stairs, but after the girl turned into the great hall the dark was almost impenetrable.

Feeling her way, she came to the door of the room, softly entered it and walked in. Passing her hands along the walls and the familiar furnishings she found the bed and lay down upon it. Her heart beat fast with excitement but not with fear. She felt thrills of hope that the ghost would appear and thrills of apprehension lest it should!

She had left the door to the hall open, and though it could scarcely be called light, there was a mitigation of the darkness near the door. A not unpleasant drowsiness overcame her, and she half slept, waking every time the clock struck in the hall.

At three, she smiled to herself, realizing that she was there, in the Room with the Tassels, and felt no fear. "I hope something comes at four," she thought sleepily, and closed her eyes again.

One—two—three—four—boomed the hall clock.

Vernie opened her eyes, only half conscious, and yet able to discern a strange chill in the air. Between her and the open door stood a tall gaunt shape, merely a shadow, for it was too dark to discern details. Her calm forsook her; she shivered violently, unable to control her muscles. Her teeth chattered, her knees knocked together, and her hair seemed to rise from her head.

Yet she could make no sound. Vainly she tried to scream, to shriek,—but her dry throat was constricted as with an iron band.

Her eyes burned in their sockets, yet she was powerless to shut them. They seemed suddenly to possess an uncanny ability to pierce the darkness, and she saw the shape draw slowly nearer to her.

Clutching the bedclothing, she tried to draw it over her head, but her paralyzed arms refused to move. Nearer, slowly nearer, the thing came, and horror reached its climax at sight of the face beneath the sheltering shawl. It was the face of a skull! The hollow eye sockets glared at her, and lifting a deathlike hand, with long white fingers, the spectre told off one, two, three, four! on the digits. There was no sound, but a final pointing of the fearsome index finger at the stricken girl, seemed a death warrant for herself.

The thing disappeared. Slowly, silently, as it had come, so it went. From nowhere to nowhere,—it evolved from the darkness and to the darkness returned.

Vernie didn't faint, but she suffered excruciatingly; her head was on fire, her flesh crept and quivered, she was bathed in a cold perspiration, and her heart beat madly, wildly, as if it would burst. The vision, though gone, remained etched on her brain, and she knew that until that faded she could not move or speak.

It seemed to her hours, but at last the tension lessened a little. The first move was agony, but by degrees she changed her position a trifle and moistened her dry lips.

With the first faint glimmer of dawn, she dragged herself upstairs and crept into bed beside Eve Carnforth.

"Tell me," begged Eve, and Vernie told her.

"It was a warning," said the child, solemnly. "It means I shall die at four o'clock some morning."

"Nonsense, Kiddie! Now you've come through so bravely, and have such an experience to tell, don't spoil it all by such croaking."

"But it's true, Eve. I could see that awful thing's face, and it counted four, and then beckoned,—sort of shook its finger, you know, and pointed at me. And—oh, I hardly noticed at the time, but it carried a glass in its hand—it seemed to have two glasses—"

"Oh, come now, dearie, you're romancing. How could it have two glasses, when it was shaking its hand at you?"

"But it did, Eve. It had two little glasses, both in the same hand. I remember distinctly. Oh, every bit of it is printed on my brain forever! I wish I hadn't done it! Rudolph told me not to!"

A flood of tears came and Vernie gave way to great racking sobs, as she buried her face in the pillow.

"Yes, he was right, too, Vernie; but you know, he only wanted you not to try it because he feared it would upset your nerves. Now if you're going to square yourself with Mr. Braye, you can only do it, by not letting your nerves be upset. So brace up and control them. Cry, dear, cry all you can. That's a relief, and will do you a heap of good. Then we'll talk it over, and by breakfast time you'll be ready to tell them all about it, and you'll be the heroine of the whole crowd. It's wonderful, Vernie, what you've got to tell, and you must be careful to tell it truly and not exaggerate or forget anything. Cry away, honey, here's a fresh handkerchief."

Eve's calm voice and matter of fact manner did much to restore Vernie's nerves, and as she looked around the rational, familiar room, bright with sunlight, her spirits revived, and she began to appreciate her role of heroine.

Her story was received with grave consideration. It was impossible to believe the honest, earnest child capable of falsehood or deceit. Her description was too realistic, her straightforward narrative too unshakable, her manner too impressively true, to be doubted in the least degree or detail.

Gifford Bruce laughed and complimented her on her pluck. Mr. Tracy reproved her for breaking her word to her cousin, but as he was in no way responsible for Vernie's behaviour, he said very little.

Landon scolded her roundly, while Milly said nothing at all.

The whole affair cast rather a gloom over them all, for it seemed as if the spectre had at last really manifested itself in earnest. An undoubted appearance to an innocent child was far more convincing than to a grown person of avowed psychic tendencies. Eve Carn forth might have imagined much of the story she told; her 'expectant attention ' might have exaggerated the facts; but Vernie's mind was like a page of white paper, on which the scene she passed through had left a clear imprint.

That night Vernie herself got out the Ouija board and asked Eve to help her try it.

"No," was the reply. "I'm too broken up. And, too, the people don't believe me. Get your uncle or Mr. Tracy or some truthful and honourable person to help you."

It embittered Eve that her earnestness and her implicit belief in the supernatural made it more difficult for the others to look upon her as entirely disingenuous. She resented this, and was a little morose in consequence. Norma Cameron, herself an avowed 'sensitive,' had had no spiritistic visitant in the haunted room, and Eve thought Norma had doubted her word.

At last after trying all the others that she wanted, Vernie persuaded good natured Mr. Tracy to move Ouija with her, and the two sat down with the board between them.

Few and flippant messages were forthcoming, until, just as Vernie had laughingly declared she would throw the old thing out of the window, a startling sentence formed itself from the erratic dartings of the heart shaped toy, and, Vernie turned pale.

"Stop it!" ordered Tracy, "I refuse to touch it again!"

He removed his hands and sat back, but Vernie, glaring at the letters, held it a moment longer. "To morrow! it says to morrow!" she cried. "Oh, Eve, I told you so!"

"What, Vernie? What is it, dear?" and Eve Carnforth came over to the excited child.

"Ouija, Eve! Ouija said that to morrow at four, two of us are to die! Oh, Eve, you know every death in this house has occurred at four o'clock in the morning! Mr. Stebbins said so. And now, two of us are to die to morrow!"

"Nonsense!" cried Mr. Tracy, "don't listen to that rubbish! The Ouija ran off its track. Maybe Vernie pushed it,—maybe I did."

"Now, Mr. Tracy, I *didn't* push it, and you needn't try to make anybody think you did! You never'd push it to say a thing like that! Why, it spelled it all out as plain as day! Uncle Gifford, do you hear! Two of us to die to morrow!" Vernie's voice rose to a hysterical shriek.

"Hush, Vernie! Hush, child. I'll take you away from here to morrow. We ought never to have brought you," and Gifford Bruce glowered at the others as he clasped the sobbing child in his arms, and took her from the room.

"You're right," agreed Mr. Tracy, "and Braye was right. He said a fright or shock would upset that child's nerves completely. But she must have pushed the board herself. It flew round like lightning, and spelled out the message, just as she said. I tried to steer it off, but she urged against me. I felt her doing so. I don't mean she made up the message to create a sensation, but I think the ghost last night affected her as a warning, and her mind is so full of it, that she unconsciously or subconsciously worked up that 'message.' At any rate, I've had about enough of this, if she's to be here. It isn't right to frighten a child so, and Vernie is little more than a child."

"That's so," said Norma, thoughtfully. "I've had enough, too. If the rest of you want to stay on, I'll go down to New York to morrow, and take Vernie to stay with me for a while. We'll go to the seashore, and I'll see to it that she has no psychic or supernatural experiences."

"Why, Norma," and Eve looked surprised, "I thought you were so interested in these things."

"So I am, but not to the extent of so affecting the nervous system of a sweet, innocent child, that it may result in permanent injury."

"She's all right," said Gifford Bruce, returning, alone. "It's hysteria. I think I'll take her back to town to morrow or next day. There's something uncanny up here, that's certain. I didn't take any stock in the experiences of you people, but I can't disbelieve Vernie's story."

The party broke up and all went to their rooms. There was no volunteer to sleep in the haunted room that night, and every one felt a shivering dread of what might happen at four o'clock the next morning.

Not one admitted it, but every one secretly shuddered at thought of Ouija's message.

And when, as the hall clock rung out its four strokes the next morning, and nothing untoward happened, every one drew a long breath and soon went to sleep again, relieved, as of a heavy burden.

Gaily they gathered at breakfast, daylight and good cheer reviving their spirits.

"But Ouija is henceforth taboo," said Mr. Tracy, shaking his finger at the now laughing
Vernie.

"For little girls, anyway," supplemented Eve.

"Little girls are taboo, also," declared Gifford Bruce. "I can't get off to day, for I want to see Rudolph on his return, but to morrow, I pack up my Vernie child and take her back to our own little old Chicago on the lake. These Aspens are too black for us!"

"Now, Uncle, I don't want to go," and Vernie pouted prettily. "And sumpum tells me I won't go," she added with a roguish glance at her uncle, whom she usually twisted round her rosy little finger.

But he gave her a grave smile in return, and the subject was dropped for the moment.

Soon after noon, Braye came up from the city, and listened, frowning, to the tales that were told him.

"You promised me, Vernie," he said, reproachfully.

"I know it, Cousin Rudolph, but you see, I've never kept a promise in my whole life,—and I didn't want to break my record!"

"Naughty Flapper! I won't give you the present I brought for you."

"Oh, yes you will," and so wheedlesome was the lovely face, and so persuasive the soft voice, that Vernie, after a short argument, seized upon a small jeweller's packet and unwrapped a pretty little ring.

"Angel Cousin," she observed, "you're just about the nicest cousin I possess,—beside being the only one!"

"Doubtful compliment!" laughed Braye. "Any way, you're the prettiest and naughtiest cousin *I* own! As a punishment for your disobedience I challenge you to a round with old Ouija to night! I'll bet I can make it say something more cheerful than you wormed out of it last evening."

"All right, we'll try it," and Vernie danced gaily away to tease her uncle not to take her home.

A little later, Milly, as housekeeper, discovered some serious shortage in the commissariat department, and Braye offered to drive her over to East Dryden, marketing.

They started off, Milly calling back to Eve to preside at the tea table, if she didn't return in time.

"All right," agreed Eve, though Vernie vociferously announced her intention of playing hostess in Milly's absence.

The shoppers had not returned when old Thorpe brought in the tea tray.

"You can pour, Eve, and I'll pass the cakies," said Vernie, who was in high spirits, for she had partially persuaded her uncle to remain longer at Black Aspens. He was just phrasing certain strong stipulations on which his permission was to be based, when the tea things arrived.

They were, as usual, in the hall, for though they sometimes suggested the plan of having tea out of doors, there was no cheerful terrace, or pleasant porch. The hall, though sombre and vast, had become more or less homelike by virtue of usage, so there they took their tea.

Mr. Tracy, always graceful in social matters, helped pass the cups and plates, for no one liked to have the old Thorpes about unnecessarily.

"No tea for me, please," declared Norma; "I think it upsets my nerves,—"

"And that is not the thing to do in *this* house," laughed Landon. "This is mighty good tea, though,—didn't know anybody could brew it as well as Milly. Congratulations, Eve."

"Thank you," and Eve's long lashes swept upward as she gave him a coquettish glance.

"Referring to that matter of which we were talking, Hardwick," Gifford Bruce began, "I—"

Even as he spoke, the clock chimed four, and, as always, they paused to count the long, slow strokes.

Then Bruce began again: "I think, myself—"

A strange change passed over his face. His jaw fell, his eyes stared, and then, his teacup fell from his hand, and he slumped down in an awful—a terrifying heap!

Landon sprang to his assistance, Norma ran to him, while Tracy, with a quick glance at Vernie, flew to the child's side.

"What is it?" he cried to her, "what's the matter, Vernie?" He slipped an arm round her, just as, with a wild look and a ringing shriek, the girl's head fell back and her eyes closed.

"Oh," cried Eve, "*what* has happened?"

"I don't know," and Tracy's voice shook. "Help me, Miss Carnforth—let us lay her on this sofa."

Between them they carried the girl, for she was past muscular effort, and as they placed her gently on the sofa her eyes fluttered, she gave a gasping sigh, and fell back, inert.

"Oh," cried Eve, "she isn't—she *isn't*—oh, it's just four o'clock!"

Landon ran to Vernie's side and felt of her heart. "She is dead," he said, solemnly, his face white, his voice shaking; "and Gifford Bruce is dead, too. It is four o'clock!"

Chapter 7: The Mystery

IN the panic stricken moments that followed the realization of the double tragedy, the natural characteristics of all those present showed themselves. Eve Carnforth, strong and calm, suddenly became self appointed dictator.

"Lay Mr. Bruce flat on his back," she called out, as she darted upstairs for her room, and returned with smelling salts, ammonia and such things.

Tracy, also capable and self possessed, took a vial from her and held it before the face of the stricken child, while others strove to bring back to consciousness the motionless figure of Gifford Bruce, now stretched on the floor.

"It's no use," declared Landon, flinging the beads of sweat from his forehead, "they are dead,—both of them. Oh, what *does* it mean?"

Norma sat in a big chair, her hands clutching its carved arms, and her face stony white. She was using all her will power to keep from utter collapse, and she couldn't understand how Eve could be so natural and self possessed.

"Brace up, Norma," Eve admonished her; "here, take this salts bottle. Now is no time to make more trouble!"

The brusque words had the effect of rousing Norma, and she forced herself to rise.

"What can I do?" she whispered.

"Do!" cried Eve, "there's everything to do! Some one telephone for a doctor!"

"I—can't," Norma moaned. "You do that, Professor,—won't you?"

"Oh, I can't!" and Hardwick fell limply into a chair. "I—I'm all upset—"

"Of course you are, Professor," said Tracy, kindly. "I'll telephone, Miss Carnforth. Do you know the village doctor's name? Of course,—it's too late—" he glanced at the two still forms, "but a physician must be summoned."

"No, I don't know any name,—call Thorpe, or Hester."

Tracy rang a bell and Thorpe came shuffling in. At sight of the tragedy, he turned and ran, screaming. Hester came, and proved the more useful of the two. Her stolidity was helpful, and she told the doctor's name and number.

"Dead, ain't they?" she said, with a grieved intonation that robbed her words of curtness. "What happened to 'em?"

The simple question roused them all. What had happened? What had killed two strong, well, able-bodied people at the same moment, and that the very moment said to be fatal in that dread house?

"I believe," said the Professor, dropping his face in his hands, "I believe now in the supernatural. Nothing else can explain this thing."

"Of course not," and Eve solemnly acquiesced. "There is no possibility of anything else. What could kill them, like this, at once, and at four o'clock exactly, except a supernormal agent?"

"But that seems so impossible!" and Tracy's practical, matter of fact voice did indeed make it seem so.

"What else is possible?" broke in Landon. "It isn't suicide, it isn't murder. It isn't death from, natural causes,—at least, it can't be in Vernie's case,—I suppose Mr. Bruce might have died from heart disease."

"That's why we want a doctor," said Eve. "We can judge nothing until we know the immediate cause of death."

"I wish we were in the city," Tracy said; "the doctor will be nearly an hour getting here, I suppose."

"Did you tell him all?" asked Eve.

"No, I didn't. It didn't seem wise to spread the news in that way. I told him to get here as soon as he possibly could,—that it was a matter of life and death."

"Which it certainly is," murmured Norma. "Oh, Eve, what do you really think?"

Eve Carn forth looked at the other girl. Eve, so poised and collected, strength and will power written in every line of her face,—Norma so fragile, and shaken by the awful scenes about her.

"I don't know what to think," Eve replied, slowly. "There's only one thing certain, Vernie received a warning of death,—and Vernie is dead. Mr. Bruce received no definite warning, that I know of, but he may have had one. You know, he said he was visited by the phantom, but we wouldn't believe him."

"That's so!" and Tracy looked up in surprise. "We never quite believed Mr. Bruce's statements, because he scorned all talk of spirit manifestations. If he really did see the ghost that night that he said he did—"

"Of course he did," declared Eve. "I believed him all the time. I can always tell when any one is speaking the truth. It's part of my sensitive nature."

Wynne Landon stalked about the hall like a man in torment. "What shall I do with Milly?" he groaned. "She and Braye will be back soon,—any minute now. She mustn't see these—"

"They ought to be placed in some other room," said Eve, gently.

"One mustn't touch a dead body before—" began Professor Hardwick, but Tracy interrupted him. "That's in case of murder, Professor," he said; "this is a different matter. Whatever caused these deaths, it wasn't by the hand of another human being. If it was fright or nervous apprehension, those are to be classed among natural causes. I think we are wholly justified in moving the bodies."

After some discussion, Landon and the Professor agreed with Tracy, and with the help of Thorpe and

Hester, the stricken forms were carried out of the hall, where the group so often forgathered.

"It is better," said Eve, "for we need this hall continually, and if we don't move them at once, the doctor may forbid it, when he comes."

By common consent, the body of Gifford Bruce was laid in the drawing room, on a large sofa, and Vernie's slender figure was reverently placed on the bed in the Room with the Tassels.

"No spirit shape can frighten her now," said Norma, weeping bitterly, as Thorpe and Hester carried the dead girl in. Then both doors were closed, shutting off the silent figures, and those who were left felt a vague sense of relief.

"Now we can break it to Milly more gently," said Eve. "Clear away that broken cup, Hester, and make some fresh tea, I'm sure we all need it."

On the great rug the damp spot remained where the spilled tea had fallen, and Eve ordered a smaller rug placed over it.

Braye and Milly came in laughing.

"We've bought out the whole of East Dryden!" Milly exclaimed, "and what do you think? We found some fresh lobsters, still alive and kicking,—and we commandeered them at once. What's the matter with you people? You look solemn as owls!"

"Come up to your room, Milly, to take off your wraps," and Landon took her arm to lead her away.

"Nonsense, Wynne, I'll throw them off down here. I'm thirsty for tea."

"No; come on, dear. Come with me."

Awed at his tone, Milly went with him, and they disappeared up the staircase.

Then Professor Hardwick told Braye what had happened. The others had begged the Professor to do this, and in a very few words the tale was told.

"It can't be!" and Braye rose and walked up and down the hall. "I wish I had been here! Oh, forgive me, all of you, I know you did all you could,—but—restoratives—"

"We did," said Eve, "I ran for sal volatile and such things, but you don't understand,—it was instantaneous,—wasn't it, Mr. Tracy?"

"It was," replied Tracy, gravely. "Mr. Bruce was speaking, naturally and normally. He paused when the clock struck,—we 'most always do, you know, it's a sort of habit."

"We have to, really," said Norma. "That clock strikes so loudly, one can't go on talking."

"And then," began the Professor, "he was talking to me, you know, and I was looking straight at him, his face changed in an instant, his fingers spread, as if galvanized, his teacup fell from his hand, and in a moment, he was gone! Yes, dead in a second, I should say."

"And—Vernie?" Braye spoke with difficulty.

"I chanced to be looking at Vernie," said Mr. Tracy. "The outcry concerning Mr. Bruce made us all look toward him, and then, a sudden sound from Vernie drew my attention to her. She gasped, and her face looked queer,—sort of drawn and gray,—so I sprang to her side, and held her up, lest she fall. She was standing, looking at Mr. Bruce, of course. I felt her sway, her head fell back, and then Miss Carnforth came to my assistance, and we laid her quickly down on the sofa. In an instant, the child was dead. It is incredible that it should have been a case of sudden fright that proved fatal, and yet, what other theory is there? It couldn't be heart disease in a child of sixteen!"

"No," mused Braye, "and yet, what could it have been? I won't subscribe to any supernatural theory now! It's too absurd!"

"It's the only thing that isn't absurd!" contradicted Eve. "Remember, Rudolph, Vernie had the warning—"

"Warning be hanged!" cried Braye, explosively.

"But think," went on Eve, gently, "the phantom told Vernie she would die at four o'clock—"

"Four o'clock in the morning, Vernie said! If I had thought of four in the afternoon, I wouldn't have gone out!"

"Nobody knows that the message said four in the morning. Vernie told me about it many times, and she only said *four*. You know, the phantom spoke no word, it merely designated by its fingers,—one, two, three, four! Also, Vernie said it carried two glasses of poison."

"But *they* weren't poisoned!"

"No; that was merely the symbol of death. Also, Rudolph, remember the Ouija board said two would die at four. You can't get away from these things!"

"That confounded Ouija performance was on one of the nights I was in New York! I wish I hadn't gone! But Vernie promised me she wouldn't sleep in that room. I was a fool to believe her. You see, Eve, I feel a sort of responsibility for the child. Uncle Gif was so easy going and indulgent,—he was no sort of a guardian for her, now she was growing up. I planned to have her put under the care of some right kind of a woman this fall, and brought up properly."

"I know it, Rudolph; you were very fond of her."

"Not only that, but I appreciated what she needed, and I meant to see that she got it. Oh, Eve, I can't realize this thing."

Doctor Wayburn came in. It was plain to be seen the man was scared. In his years of country practice he had never run up against anything tragic or thrilling before, and he was overwhelmed. With trembling step he entered the room of death, and first made examination of the body of Gifford Bruce. It did not take long. There was no apparent cause for death. No symptoms were present of any fatal disease, nor, so far as he could see, of any poison or wound of any sort.

"I cannot say what an autopsy may divulge," declared the frightened practitioner, "but from this superficial examination, I find no cause of dissolution."

Then he crossed the hall, to the Room with the Tassels.

Braye followed him in, Eve also. The Professor and Tracy stood in the doorway, but Norma remained in the hall, her face buried in some sofa cushions.

"No apparent cause," the Doctor repeated. "This child was in perfect health; I should say fright *might* have killed her, but it doesn't seem credible. I know of no cause of any sort, that could bring about death in an instant of time, as you report."

"Maybe not an instant," corrected the Professor, carefully. "As I look back, I should judge there was at least a half a minute between Mr. Bruce's first symptom of unease, and his falling to the floor."

"So with Vernie," said Eve, thoughtfully. "I saw Mr. Tracy go quickly toward her; I followed immediately, and I'm sure there was nearly a half minute, but not more, before she gasped and died."

"It's hard to judge time on such occasions," said the Doctor, looking sharply at Eve.

"I know it, but I was very conscious of it all, almost clairvoyantly so, and I can assure you it was not longer than a half minute in either case, between the state of usual health and death itself. Is there any cause or agent that will work as quickly as that?"

"I know of none," replied Doctor Wayburn, positively.

"There is none," Eve assured him. "These deaths were caused by supernatural means, they were the vengeance of certain Powers of Darkness."

"Oh, come now, Eve," expostulated Braye, "don't get off that stuff to the Doctor. Keep that for our own circle. You know these fatalities *couldn't* have been caused by a ghost!"

"What, then?"

"I don't know. Fright, perhaps, or over apprehension because of the warnings. Auto suggestion, if you like, and so indirectly the result of the spooks, but not the direct work of a disembodied spirit."

"It was, all the same!" and Eve left the room and went to sit by Norma.

But the girls were not in sympathy. Their conversation resulted in disagreement, and, at last, in Norma's bursting into tears and running upstairs. She sought Milly, and found her prostrated by Landon's news. But she was trying to be brave, and earnestly endeavouring to preserve her self control.

"I know every one thinks I'll go to pieces," she said, pathetically, "and make more trouble for you all,—but I won't. I've promised Wynne I'll be brave and if I can't keep quiet and composed, I'll stay in my room, and not upset the crowd."

"You're all right, Milly," Norma reassured her, "you let yourself go all you want to. Don't overdo your restraint. I'll look after you."

"Yes, do, Norma. Don't let Eve come near me. I can't stand her!"

"Why? You mustn't be unjust to Eve. She behaved splendidly at that awful time."

"Yes, I know. But if it hadn't been for Eve we never would have come up here at all."

"Oh, Milly, that isn't fair! We all agreed to come here. It wasn't Eve's doing any more than mine!"

"Yes, it was. But, look here, Norma, tell me truly. What do you think killed Mr. Bruce and Vernie?"

"I don't know, Milly, dear. You know I do believe in psychics and in spiritism and in the return to earth of the souls of people who have died, but–I *can't* believe that any such spirit would kill an innocent child, or a fine old man. I can't *believe* it!"

"But why not, Norma? If you believe in the return to earth of good spirits, why not bad spirits, as well? And if so, why couldn't they kill people, if they want to?"

"You sound logical, Milly, but it's absurd."

"No, it isn't. You and Eve believe in good spirits and in their power to do good. Why not, then, in bad spirits and their power to do evil?"

"Let up, Milly," begged Landon, who stood near by. "She's been going on like that, Norma, ever since I told her. Can't you explain to her—"

"Explain what?"

"Lord! I don't know! But make her see how impossible it is that the ghost of that woman who killed her husband here so long ago, should have any reason to do away with two modern present day people!"

"But I *want* to think so, Wynne," and Milly's eyes stared with a peculiar light. "I'd rather think they were killed by that ghost than by a person,—wouldn't you?"

"What do you mean, Milly? Murdered?"

"Yes, Eve. That's what it must have been, if not spirits. They had no mortal disease, either of them."

"Don't mention that before any one else," admonished Eve, very seriously. "There are other explanations, Milly. Many deaths have been brought about by sudden fright or by continuous apprehension of imaginary danger. Vernie had been warned twice. True, I didn't think of four in the afternoon, but doubtless she did, and maybe, seeing the sudden attack of Mr. Bruce, so startled her that she thought of the four o'clock doom and gave way herself."

"She might give way to the extent of fainting, or a fit of hysterics," admitted Milly, "but not to the extent of dropping dead! It's unthinkable,—it's unbelievable—"

"It's almost unbelievable that they should be dead," Eve said, softly, "but as to how they died, let's not speculate, dear. I suppose we must have a doctor up from New York,—what do you think, Mr. Landon?"

"Eh?—oh, I don't know,—I'm sure I don't know."

"But you'll have to take charge, won't you?" asked Eve. "You two are really the heads of this house—"

"All I want is to get away," moaned Milly. "When can we go, Wynne?"

"I don't know, dear. Say, Eve, won't you take Milly down to night? I can't leave, of course, but I daren't keep her here, lest she go to pieces. You take her home,—there's a train in about an hour."

"Oh, I can't. I want to stay here. Send Norma,—no, she's no good,—perhaps Mr. Tracy will take Milly down. He's awfully kind, and ready to do anything."

As Milly declared herself now willing, the three went downstairs. They found the others in the hall, the Doctor still there, and the tea things still about. Eve gave Milly some tea, and took some herself.

"I'll have to call in the coroner," Doctor Wayburn was saying; "it isn't apparently a murder, and yet it's a mysterious death,—they both are. Yes, the county physician must be summoned."

The Doctor had gotten over the first panic of surprise, and began to feel a sense of importance. Such a case had never come near him before, and the whole affair gave him a pleasant feeling of responsibility and foreshadowed his prominence in the public eye.

The suggestion of a coroner was resented by all who listened, but the Doctor's word was law in the case, so they unwillingly consented.

"I think I'd better go down to New York tonight," said Braye. "There are so many things to see to, so many people to notify, the reporters to look after, and—undertaking arrangements to be made. Unless you want to go, Wynne?"

"No," said Landon, "it's better for you, Rudolph. But I wish you'd take Milly. Take her to her mother's and let her get out of this atmosphere. Will you go, Milly?"

"I did want to, Wynne, when I was upstairs. But, now, with people all about,—if Norma will stay here, too, I'd rather stay with you. When are you going down, Wynne?"

"I don't know, dear. We'll have to see how things turn out. Well, you go ahead, Rudolph, you'll have to hustle to get over to the train. And there are a few matters I wish you'd look after for me."

The two men went off to discuss these matters, and then Doctor Wayburn, who had been telephoning, announced that the coroner could not come until the next day, as he was in another township attending to some duties.

"And I'm glad of it," said Eve, "for we've had enough excitement for one day."

And so, by ten or eleven o'clock, the house was locked up and the members of the household gone to bed, all except old Thorpe, who sat in the great hall, with the two doors open into the rooms where the still, tragic figures lay. Before him, on a table, Hester had placed coffee and sandwiches, and the old man sat, brooding on the awful events of the afternoon.

Chapter 8: By What Means

THE night was full of restlessness. Tracy and Professor Hardwick, in their adjoining rooms, were the only ones in the wing that had the night before also housed Braye and Gifford Bruce.

"Shall we leave the door between open?" Tracy asked, more out of consideration for the Professor's nerves than his own.

"Yes, if you will. And don't go to bed yet. I can't sleep, I know, and I must discuss this thing with somebody, or go mad!"

"All right, sir," and Tracy took off his coat and donned an old fashioned dressing gown.

Hardwick smiled. "That's the first ministerial garb I've seen you wear," he said. "I'd pick that up for a dominie's neglige every time!"

"I'm rather attached to the old dud," and Tracy patted it affectionately. "Queer, how one comes to love a worn garment. No, I don't wear clerical togs when off on a vacation. I used to, till some one told me it cast a restraint over the others, and I hate to feel I'm doing that."

"You'd never do that, my friend. You've a natural tact that ought to carry you far toward general popularity. But, tell me, as man to man, how do you size up this awful mystery?"

"I don't know, Professor. At times my mind's a blank,—and then, I get a hint or,—well, I can't call it a suspicion,—but a thought, say, in one direction, and it's so fearfully absurd, I discard it at once. Then comes another idea, only to be dismissed like the first. What do you think?"

"I am a complete convert to the supernatural. You know, Sir Oliver Lodge and many other scientists only believed after they had had undeniable personal experience. Now, here were warnings,—definite, positive prophecies, and they were fulfilled. What more can any one ask?"

Tracy mused over this. "I know that," he said, at last, "but I can't quite swallow it whole, like that. Do you mean there was no physical cause? Such as fright, expectant attention,—"

"Expectant attention is a fine phrase,—much like auto suggestion. They are all right as far as they go, but they can't go to the extent of killing people. Then again, suggest even a theory, even a possible means of the death of those two by any human agency. Murder is out of the question,—suicide even more so. And they had no desire to end their lives. A young girl, happily looking forward to gaiety and pleasure,—a man in the prime of life, hale, rich, prosperous—no, they had no wish to die!"

"True enough; but I can't quite see it. Why did the spirits want to kill them? if spirits did kill them?"

"For interfering with this haunted house,—in a frivolous and flippant way. I've always heard that departed souls bitterly resent scoffing, or merely curious investigation."

"But why choose those two? Or Vernie, anyway? Perhaps Mr. Bruce was needlessly sarcastic and sceptical."

"So was the child—"

"Oh, but in such an innocent, harmless way! However, Professor, I've nothing to offer in place of your argument. My creed does not admit of my subscribing to your theory, but I confess I'm unable to suggest any other. As you say, it couldn't have been suicide, and there's no possibility of foul play."

The two men talked on, or sat in silent thought, far into the night. The clock struck twelve before they at last retired, leaving open their communication door, and securely locking their hall doors.

Less than an hour later, a slender white robed figure tiptoed from one of the bedrooms and looked over the banisters. Peering down through the darkness, the dim outline of old Thorpe's form was visible. He was huddled in his chair, his head fallen forward on the table. Softly returning to her room for a wrap, Eve again stealthily came to the staircase, and sat down on the uppermost step.

Later still, another door silently opened, and a pair of surprised blue eyes saw Eve sitting there.

Suppressing a startled exclamation, Norma scurried back to her room, but Eve did not hear her.

Milly was wakeful and restless. Several times she declared she heard sounds, but when Wynne wanted to go and investigate, she refused to let him do so.

The house surely seemed haunted. The aspens brushed against the windows with their eternal soughing, their leaves whispering,—hissing creepy secrets, and their branches tapping eerily on the panes. The halls were full of shadows, vague, indistinct, fading to nothingness.

At four o'clock the great clock tolled the hour, and every one in the house heard it. No one was asleep, every heart was beating fast, every eye wide open, every nerve tense.

But nothing happened; no shriek rent the silence, no unusual or terrifying sound was heard.

Relieved, some went to sleep again, some tossed restlessly on their pillows until rising time.

At breakfast all looked haggard and worn. The day was cool and pleasant, the dining room bright with sunshine, and old Hester's viands most appetizing.

Thorpe had closed the doors of the rooms given over to the presence of death, and as the various members of the party came down the staircase quick apprehensive glances were followed by a look of relief.

Elijah Stebbins came while breakfast was in progress, and at Milly's invitation took a seat at the board.

"Well," he said heavily, "you folks wanted spooks, I hope you're satisfied."

"Don't use that tone, Mr. Stebbins," Landon reproved him. "A dreadful thing has happened. I cannot think it is by supernatural causes nor can I see any other explanation. But that is no reason for you to speak flippantly of our investigations of your so called haunted house."

"No offence meant," and Stebbins cringed. "But I'm thinkin' you folks had better go away from here, or there's no tellin' what might happen."

"Do you know anything about the mystery?" Professor Hardwick shot out the question so suddenly that Stebbins jumped.

"No, sir, of course I don't, sir! How could I?"

"Then why do you warn us off the premises?"

"I don't exactly do that, but I'd think you'd reason for yourselves that what happens once can happen ag'in."

The dogged look on the man's face seemed portentous of evil, and Milly began to cry.

"Oh, take me home, Wynne," she begged; "I don't want to stay here!"

"Come with me, Milly," said Eve, and rising, she led Milly from the room.

It was shortly after that the coroner arrived.

"I don't want to see that man," said Stebbins, "him and me ain't good friends," and rising quickly, the owner of the house fled toward the kitchen quarters, and spent the rest of the morning with the Thorpes out there.

Doctor Crawford, the county physician and coroner, was a man of slow speech and dignified manner. He was appalled by the circumstances in which he found himself, and a little frightened at the hints he had heard of ghostly visitations.

Indeed, that had been the real reason for his delay in arriving,—he had not been willing to brave the darkness of the night before. This was his secret, however, and his excuse of conflicting duties had been accepted.

The whole party gathered in the hall to hear what the newcomer had to say.

Eve and Milly returned, the latter, quivering and tearful, going straight to her husband's side, and sitting close to him.

Norma was pale and trembling, too, and Tracy's watchful eye regarded her sympathetically, as he led her to a seat.

Eve, self reliant and calm, flitted about incessantly. She went to the kitchen and talked over household matters with Hester, for Milly was unable to do this. Then, returning, Eve went into the drawing room, and after a few moments returned, closing the door again after her. Then she stepped into the Room with the Tassels. She was there longer, but at last came out, and locking the door behind her, retained the key. No one noticed this but Norma, and she kept her own counsel, but she also kept a watchful eye on Eve.

Even before he went to look at the bodies of the two victims of the tragedy, Doctor Crawford asked some questions.

His slowness was maddening to the alert minds of his listeners, but he methodically arrived at the facts of the case.

"I am told by my colleague, Doctor Wayburn," he said, "that there is no mark or sign on the remains to indicate the cause of death. There will, of course, be need of autopsies, but for that I will await Doctor Wayburn's return. He will be here shortly. Meantime, I will inquire concerning this strange information I have received, hinting at a belief in—ahem—in spiritualism, by some of the people here present. Is such belief held, may I ask?"

"Perhaps belief is too strong a word," the Professor volunteered, as no one else spoke, "but I may tell you that we came here to this house for the purpose of investigating the truth of the story that the house is haunted."

"And have you made such investigations?"

"We have tried to do so. The results have been mysterious, startling and now,—tragic,—but I cannot say we have proved anything, except that supernatural influences have most assuredly been at work."

"I am not willing to accept such an explanation of two sudden deaths," Crawford said, in his dignified way, "at any rate, not without a most exhaustive investigation into the possibility of their having been brought about by natural agencies. Let me take up first the case of Mr. Bruce. Was this gentleman in robust health?"

"Entirely so," said Landon, "so far as we know. It is not inconceivable that he had some heart trouble or other malady that was not noticeable, but of that I cannot say positively. It seems to me, Doctor, you would better look at him, you might note some symptom that would enlighten you."

Crawford shuddered perceptibly, but tried to hide his disinclination. Though accustomed to gruesome sights, his dread of the supernatural was such that he feared the proposed examination. However, ashamed of his hesitation, he rose, and asked to be shown the body of Gifford Bruce.

Landon started to officiate, but Milly's detaining hand held him back; the Professor made no move, but Eve and Tracy started simultaneously to rise.

"I'll go," said Eve, a little officiously, and Tracy sat down again.

She led the way to the big drawing room, where the remains of Gifford Bruce lay, and stood by while Doctor Crawford looked down at the still, white face.

A long time they stood there, no word being spoken. Then Eve said softly, "Don't let your disbelief in supernatural powers blind you to their possible reality. There are many matters yet unknown and spiritism is one of them. Remember that we who are here gathered are sensitives and psychics. We are prepared for and expect experiences not vouchsafed to less clairvoyant natures,—though we did not look for *this!* But I beg of you, sir, to realize that there are things of which you have no cognizance, that yet are real and effective."

Doctor Crawford looked at the speaker. In the partially darkened room, Eve's strange eyes glittered with an uncanny light. Her face was pale, and her red hair like a flame aureole. She took a slow step nearer to the doctor, and he recoiled, as from a vampire.

"You are afraid!" she said, and her tone was exultant. "Do not be afraid,—the phantasms will not hurt you if you do your duty. Unless you do your duty–" she stretched her hand toward him, and again he drew away, "the phantasms will haunt you–*haunt* you–*haunt* you!"

Her voice fell to the merest whisper, but it thrilled through the room like a clarion note to the shocked ears of the listening man.

Against his will her eyes held his; against his will, without his volition, he whispered, "What *is* my duty?"

"To declare,—to declare in accordance with your own conviction, in proof of your own belief,—that these two deaths were the direct result of a supernatural power. What power, you know not, but you do know—remember, you *do* know, that no mortal hand brought the tragedy about, either the hands of the victims themselves or of any one else."

Fascinated, frightened, Crawford stared at this strange woman. He had never before encountered such a face, such a sinuous, serpentine form, a personality that seemed to sway his very being, that seemed to dominate and control his whole will power, his whole brain power.

"Don't misunderstand me," Eve went on, "don't think for a moment, I am advising you wrongly, or with intent to deceive. Only, I see you know nothing of occult phenomena, and moreover, you are even ignorant of your own ignorance of them. Therefore, seeing, too, your quick appreciation and perceptive faculty, I warn you not to ignore or forget the fact that these things exist, that unseen powers hold sway over us all, and they must be reckoned with."

The flattery was subtle. More than the words, Eve's glance implied a keen apprehension on the part of the doctor, which, as he didn't possess it, seemed a desirable thing to him, and he gladly assumed that he had it.

"And now," Eve said, as they left the room, "do you want to go to the other room—the Room with the Tassels?"

"No—please, not now," and Crawford shuddered, for he had heard much of that room. Also, he was desirous of getting back to more normal associates than this strange being, and he resolved to leave the examination of the other victim until the return of his fellow physician, who at least was practical, and an unbeliever in spooks.

Shaken by the whole episode, Doctor Crawford concealed his disquiet by a manner even more slow and deliberate than usual. He said no word of Gifford Bruce, but announced his desire to ask a few general questions concerning practical matters.

"Where is your home, Mr. Landon?" he inquired, and then asked the same question of each.

He learned that they were all residents of New York City, except Mr. Tracy, who had lived in Philadelphia, but was contemplating a move to New York.

"I have had a call to a pastorate there," Tracy stated, "and it seems advisable to me to accept it."

"Mr. Bruce lived in Chicago, did he not?" went on Crawford, "and Miss Reid, also?"

"Yes," said Landon, "but Miss Reid had been at school in Connecticut for the last three years. She was graduated in June, and her uncle and guardian, Mr. Bruce, came East for the occasion. They concluded to spend the summer with us, intending to return to Chicago next month."

"Mr. Bruce was a wealthy man?" inquired the questioner.

"Yes;" answered Landon, "not a financial magnate, but worth at least two million dollars."

"And who are his heirs?"

The question fell like a bombshell. It had not been thought of, or at least not spoken of, by any of the party. The bareness of it, the implication of it, gave a shock, as of a sudden accusation.

"I hadn't thought of that," Wynne Landon said, slowly.

"But you know?" queried Crawford.

"Of course I know. Unless Gifford Bruce left a contradictory will, his estate must revert to Rudolph Braye, the son of Mr. Bruce's half brother—"

"Why, Wynne," interrupted Milly, "you're a cousin."

"I am," and Landon flushed unaccountably, "but I'm a second cousin. Braye would inherit, unless a will made other proviso."

"Where is Mr. Braye?"

"He went to New York last evening and has not yet returned."

"You expect him soon?"

"This afternoon, probably. Of course, he has realized that he is the heir of a great fortune, but naturally he would not discuss it last evening, when we were all so alarmed and excited over the awfulness of the situation."

"Was Mr. Braye present at the time of the—tragedy?"

"No," Landon stopped to think. "He wasn't. Where was he?"

"He was with me," said Milly. "We went in his car to East Dryden. We went to the markets and did some other shopping at the stores."

"And when you returned it was—all over?" Doctor Crawford looked gravely at her.

"Yes," said Milly, "we were both away, and oh, I am so glad! I couldn't have stood it!"

She broke down and sobbed in her husband's arms, but Crawford went on asking questions.

"The autopsy will show," he said, "but I will ask if any of you can show cause to suspect that a poison of any sort could have been administered to the victims of this disaster."

"Not possibly," said Professor Hardwick. "We were at tea, and had all been served from the same teapot and from the same plates of cakes. I can affirm this, for I've thought over every moment of the occasion. Mr. Bruce had taken part of his tea, and had eaten part of his cake,—"

"Are you sure of this?" the coroner interrupted.

"I am sure that he sat next to me, that he was talking to me, and that he received his tea at the same time I did. We sat stirring our cups, and nibbling our cake as we discussed a matter in which we were both interested. Less than a half minute before that man died, he was as well as he had ever been. The scene is perfectly before my eyes. He held his cup and saucer in one hand, his spoon in the other,—when I saw his eyes open queerly, his face change to a clayey gray, and his fingers relaxed, letting his cup fall to the floor. I set down my cup quickly and sprang toward him, but in an instant it was all over."

A hush fell on the group as all remembered the details, so exactly as the Professor had related them.

"And the young lady," said Crawford, at last, rousing himself from thought, "did she too drink tea?"

"No," said Eve Carn forth, musingly. "I remember I was just fixing Vernie's tea. She liked it sweet, and I was adding a lump of sugar when the commotion began."

"I noticed Miss Reid first, I think," offered Tracy; "at least, I happened to look toward her when Mr. Bruce fell forward in his chair. She made a slight sound, as of horror, and when I glanced her way, she looked so stunned I thought she was going to collapse, so I stepped across toward her. As I did so, she looked suddenly very strange, and I feared she was ill,—aside from her shock at sight of Mr. Bruce. I grasped her by the shoulders just as she was about to fall. She cried out as if in pain, and then Miss Carn forth came to my assistance, and we laid the child on that sofa. In an instant, she, too, was gone."

"She had taken no tea?"

"No," said Eve, positively. "Nor any cakes. As a rule, the elders were served first and Vernie last. So there is no chance of there having been poison in the tea or cakes,— nor could it be possible, anyway, as we all ate them,— didn't we?"

Every one present affirmed that they had partaken of the tea and the cakes, and declared they were both harmless and just such as they had had served every afternoon since their arrival.

"That settles that point, at any rate," and the coroner nodded his head. "There can be no question of poison after what you've told me. Unless, either or both of them took poison themselves or gave it to the other intentionally."

Chapter 9: Conflicting Theories

IN the kitchen the discussion was going on in less guarded terms.

"It's murder," Thorpe declared flatly. "No spooks ever killed off those two people in a minute, just like that!"

"Murder, your grandmother!" snorted Stebbins. "Who done it, and how? I ask you that! Those folks came up here to hunt ghosts, and I should say they found 'em, good and plenty! You know's well's I do, this house has always been ha'nted, ever since that woman killed her husband in that very room where the little girl's lyin' now. I wouldn't go in that there room for a fortune, I wouldn't!"

"Now Eli, don't be foolish," and Thorpe shook his head. "How could a spook kill two folks at onct,—right out in the open, as you may say?"

"For that matter, how could anybody murder two people at once? Nobody was around but their own crowd, and that lot of people ain't for murderin' each other! I know that!"

"It was spooks," declared Hester, with an air of settling the matter; "I've smelled 'em of late. That smell of bitter almonds is been in the air a heap, and I ain't had none for flavourin' or anything. Land, I'd never flavour a cake with that! I put vanilla even in my 'Angel Food.'"

"I've smelled it too," spoke up Nannie, a helper of the older woman's; "when I've been a dustin' round in that there ha'nted room, I've smelled it—not strong, you know, but jest a faint whiff, now'n then. I skittled out 's fast's I could, I kin tell you!"

"Nope, you're all wrong," insisted old Thorpe. "'Tain't spooks, it's murder. That's what it is."

"Who done it, then?" demanded his wife.

"That I dunno. But I have my s'picions. How,—I dunno, either. But that's neither here nor there. Murder's been done, but I'll bet that mutton headed Crawford ain't got brains enough to see it."

"He ain't got brains enough to go in when it rains," agreed Stebbins, "but you're 'way off,

Thorpe, a surmisin' murder. Why, jest f'r instance, now, how *could* it 'a' been done?"

"Now how can I tell that!" Thorpe spoke with fine scorn. "I don't know all the goin's on of them hifalutin folks, but if you'd heard 'em talkin' 's much as I have, you'd know that they're up to lots of things such as us ignorant people don't know nothin' about."

"They do talk awful hifalutin," corroborated Hester. "I've heard 'em say things that hadn't no meanin' whatsoever to me, and yet they was plain English too."

"Well, if you ask me," and Thorpe looked important, "I'd jest say keep your eye on one of them women."

"You mean that red headed varmint, I know," said his wife. "Well, she's a handful, all right, but I don't believe she'd go so far's to kill anybody."

"You don't, don't you? Well, she'd go just so far as there was any goin' at all,—an' then she'd go right on. Oh, I kin read character," and Thorpe plumed himself so evidently on his mental powers that Stebbins snorted outright.

"You're, a hummer, you are! I s'pose you're clairvoyant, yourself! Well, let me advise you to keep your trap shut about Miss—that lady you referred to. This is my house, and those are my tenants, and I won't stand any talk from you about 'em."

"That's right, Thorpe," admonished his wife. "Mr. Stebbins, he's right. An' he's right about the ghosts, too. Why, I happen to know that the spooks warned that little Reid girl she'd die at four o'clock, and die she did, jest at four! Can you beat it? Spooks? Why, of course it was spooks! What else?"

"Yes, and the message was that two of 'em 'd die, and two of 'em did," added Stebbins. "How could any mortal human bein' bring that about? I ask you?"

"Land! I don't know! I told you I didn't. But," and Thorpe wagged his head positively, "it wasn't spooks."

The same questions were being discussed in the hall by the ones more intimately interested.

Doctor Wayburn had arrived, and he and Crawford were shut in the drawing room endeavouring to wrest from the unknown, the secret of Gifford Bruce's death.

The little group, still gathered in the hall, were talking earnestly of the immediate future.

"It's so pathetic," Norma was saying, "that there are so few to mourn for poor little Vernie. That child had actually no relatives but her uncle and Mr. Braye."

"Wynne is a sort of a cousin, too," put in Milly, "and indeed, Norma, I feel as sorry as if Vernie had been my own sister."

"Oh, I don't mean that,—of course, we all feel that way. But, she was so alone in the world. Mr. Braye is terribly broken up. He loved her—"

"Not only loved her," said Eve, "but he was ambitious for her. He wanted her put in care of a capable woman this fall, and brought up properly. Mr. Bruce was no sort of a guardian for the child—I mean he was all right, of course, as a legal guardian, but he was no man to have charge of her social and home life."

"He knew that," said Landon, "he told me he meant to have Vernie properly chaperoned and all that, this winter. She was a dear kiddie."

"Oh, she was," and Norma wept afresh.

"I am a complete convert to spiritualism, now," said the Professor, gravely. "I've thought over these things very deeply, I've considered every possible aspect of the case, and there is no explanation of those two mysterious deaths, except supernormal forces. It is no use to shirk the supposition of murder, indeed we must consider it very carefully, but it is out of the question. Nobody could have compassed those two deaths in an instant of time, however secret or subtle the methods. Do you all agree?"

"Of course," said Eve, positively, and Tracy added, "That is undeniable, Professor, foul play was impossible. But, moreover, there was no one here present but our own party. I can't let the implication pass that it could have been in the heart of any one of us—"

"Nonsense!" interrupted Hardwick, "that's absurd, Mr. Tracy. When I speak of murder, it is in the abstract, and because it is right that we should consider the matter from every angle. We must even think of suicide, and of—"

"Suicide is as absurd as murder," said Landon, indignantly. "But what other atrocity had you in mind?"

"Don't lose your temper, please," the Professor said, mildly. "I am obliged to preserve an impersonal attitude, or I can't think at all! The other thought is, that one of the victims killed himself and the other one."

"Please, Professor," said Eve, "at least confine yourself to rational common sense. But since you raise this absurd theory, let's settle it once and for all. Could Mr. Bruce nave willingly killed himself and Vernie?" she asked of them all.

"No!" replied Landon. "Mr. Bruce was fond of life and he adored that child! Cut that out!"

"Then," pursued Eve, "could Vernie have killed herself and her uncle?"

"Rubbish!" cried Landon, "don't say such things, Eve. Professor, are you answered?"

"And remember," put in Tracy, "the two were the width of this hall apart. What means could have been employed?"

"What means were employed, anyway?" said Norma. "Oh, what did kill those people?"

"The utter absence of any material means proves the fact that it was supernatural," declared the Professor. "I only mentioned those other theories to prove their absurdity. Now, as I say, I am a convert to spiritualism in all its form and phases. How can one help being after this? And I, for one, desire to stay here for a time and I feel sure that the departed spirits of our friends will communicate with us."

Milly shuddered at the idea, but Eve's wonderful eyes glowed with a sudden anticipation.

"Oh, Professor Hardwick!" she exclaimed, "how splendid! Will you really stay here a while? Will you, Milly? I can't stay unless you and Wynne do. Will you stay, Norma? and you, Mr. Tracy?"

"Oh, I can't!" Milly moaned. "I needn't, need I, Wynne?"

"No; darling, not if you don't want to. I can't see, Eve, why you wish to stay here. It gives me the horrors to think of it. And if you really expect spiritual communications from Vernie or Mr. Bruce, you can receive them just as well anywhere else."

"Not just as well," demurred the Professor. "The conditions here are ideal for investigations. We haven't taken it up seriously, you know."

"But, Miss Carnforth, can't you ask some other friends to come, if the Landons prefer to return to New York? I don't doubt you know the right ones, who could chaperon you, and also take an interest in our work."

"Yes," began Eve, thoughtfully, and then Stebbins came into the room.

"The doctors through yet?" he asked; "what they found out?"

"No, they're not through yet," answered Landon. "Sit down, Stebbins, and talk a little bit. I wish you'd tell us of anything you know of your own experience, not hearsay, mind you, that has happened in this house, that can truly be called supernatural."

"Well, that ha'nted room,—"

"Wait a minute," interrupted Landon, "don't tell us anything about that haunted room that you don't *know*, personally, to be a fact."

"I know it's ha'nted," asserted Stebbins, doggedly. "I've slept there and I've seen ghosts spookin' around in it."

"Do you think there are really such things as ghosts?"

"I know it."

"And do you think they could be responsible for the death of Mr. Bruce and Miss Reid?"

"I know it. That Thorpe he says it's murder, but he can't guess how it could be. That fool of a Crawford, he don't know nothing, of any sort. Wayburn, now, he's a fair doctor, but, good land! what can they learn from a post mortem? Those people was warned, and them warnin's was carried out. What more is there to learn?"

"Well and clearly put, Mr. Stebbins," commented the Professor. "No elaboration of phrases could state that more succinctly. They were warned,—the warnings were carried out. That is the whole truth."

"But granting that," said Norma, "and I'm willing to grant it, why did the spirits want to kill Vernie? A lovely, innocent child couldn't have incurred the wrath of the spirits to that extent."

"They ain't no tellin', ma'am, what them ha'nts wll do." Stebbins spoke heavily, as if burdened with fear. "Now I leave it to you folks. Ain't you smelled prussic acid around?"

"I have," said Norma. "And I," added the Professor. "I know it was not brought here by any of our party "

"Nor not by the cook," said Stebbins. "Hester, she's leery of that bitter almond flavourin' and she don't never use it. Well, don't that smell prove somethin' ?"

"It isn't actual proof," and Tracy looked thoughtful. "But it is an inexplicable odour to hang round an old house."

"'Tain't inexplicable if it's due to the ha'nt," urged Stebbins. "And that's what it is due to. Why, that smell's been said to be round here ever since the time of the Montgomery murder."

"What's wrong between you and Doctor Crawford?" asked Eve, suddenly. "You say yourself you aren't good friends."

"No, ma'am, we ain't. It's a sort o' feud of long standin'. They ain't no special reason, jest a conglomeration of little things. But one thing is 'cause he makes fun of the spooks here. He don't take no stock in such things, and nobody can make him. Thorpe, now, he don't neither. He sticks to it Mr. Bruce and Miss Vernie was murdered."

"By what means, does he think?" asked Eve, quickly.

"Well, that he don't know. But murder he says it was, and that he sticks to, like a puppy to a root."

"Get him in here," said Landon, abruptly, and Thorpe was summoned.

"Yes, sir," the butler averred, on being questioned. "I'm willin' to go on record as a disbeliever in spooks. They ain't no such things. I don't deny I've been some scared up hearin' you ladies and gentlemen talk about such matters. But I don't believe in 'em and I never will. Them two pore critters was done to death, but I'm free to confess I can't see how."

Professor Hardwick looked at the speaker. "As Mr. Dooley observed," he said, "your remarks is inthrestin' but not convincin'. My man, if there is no possible way that murder could have been done,—and we in here are agreed on that point,—what is left but the inevitability of supernormal agents?"

"Your long words gets me, sir, but it don't make no difference. It wa'n't spooks."

"He's hopeless," said Tracy. "Let's ask him other things. Thorpe, my man, have you never seen any circumstance or occurrence in this house, that you couldn't explain by natural means?"

"I ain't never been in this house, sir, except as I came here to buttle for you folks. Mr. Stebbins, he give the job to me and my wife, 'cause we're honest, hard working people, and he knew he could trust us not to tattle or tell no tales of your goin's on. He says, 'Thorpe,' says he, 'they're a queer lot what's comin' up here, but they're my tenants, and I don't want 'em bothered none by gossip and tale bearin' to the village.' Ain't that right, Mr. Stebbins?"

"Just so," said Stebbins, calmly. "Them's just about my very words. You told me, Mr. Landon, that you were a crowd of spook hunters, and so it was up to me to spare you all the annoyance I could. An' well I know how the villagers gossip about this here house, if they get a chance. So, with the Thorpes at the head of things and a couple of good close mouthed girls for helpers, I 'llowed you'd not be troubled. And you ain't been,—up to now. But this thing can't be kept quiet no longer. Of course, a thing like this is more or less public property, and I can tell you, there'll be plenty of curious villagers up here to the inquest and all that."

"Inquest!" cried Eve, "what do you mean?"

"Jest that, ma'am. That dunder headed coroner, or county physician as he really is, he's set on havin' an inquest,—says he's got to. Well, I don't know much about law, but if they can ketch and hang a ha'nt, let 'em do it, say I!"

The arrival on the scene of the two doctors cut short further discussion. "There is a strange condition of things," Crawford began, addressing himself to Wynne Landon. "We find decisive, though very slight evidence that Mr. Bruce died from poison."

A hush followed, as his stunned hearers thought over the grave significance of this statement.

"Poison?" repeated Landon. dazedly. "What sort of poison? Who administered it?"

"As I said," resumed the coroner, "it's a strange case. The poison found is the minutest quantity of a very powerful drug, known among the profession as strychnine hydrochlorate. This is so deadly that a half grain will kill a man instantly, or in a few seconds. But my colleague and I have agreed that since it is impossible for this to have been administered at the moment of Mr. Bruce's death, it must be that he had taken it in cumulative doses, and the result culminated in his sudden death."

"Why would he take it?" cried Milly. "Where could he get it?" asked the Professor.

"Such a drug is not available to the general public, is it?"

"It is not, sir, but whoever gave it to him, must have procured it somehow. Those questions are for the future. We are just learning the facts. The results of our tests prove positively the presence of that particular poison. There is no doubt of that."

"But wait," and Eve fixed her compelling eyes on the coroner's face. "Remember, Doctor Crawford, though you may not believe in the occult, other and wiser minds do. I wish to remind you, therefore, that we who believe these deaths were caused by supernatural agency, believe also that the powers that compassed the deaths are able to make the deaths seem attributable to natural causes, whether poison or anything else."

"Eve!" exclaimed Milly, "that is going too far!"

"Not at all!" said the Professor. "Miss Camforth is quite right; and indeed, logic must prove that if a phantasm can take away a human life it can also produce effects that resemble conditions brought about by human means."

"I repeat," the coroner interrupted, "these things are beside the question. We are conducting an autopsy, not an inquest, at present. I am giving you my report as a medical man, not as a member of the police force. Those other matters will be considered later. We have completed our examinations in the one case, we will now proceed to the case of the other victim."

"They killed each other," Thorpe broke in, nodding his head in the positive manner he affected. "Leastwise, one of 'em killed both; and of course, Miss Vernie, she wasn't no murderer!"

"Wait till you are called upon to testify, my man," and Crawford glowered at the forwardness of the old butler.

"There'll be testifyin' on both sides," volunteered Stebbins, speaking a little belligerently.

Crawford turned on him, and it was easily seen that enmity existed between these two. "You, 'Lijah Stebbins, keep quiet," he admonished, "there's them that says you know too much about these doings, anyhow."

"What do you mean by that?" Stebbins' eyes glowed with anger.

"Nothing now, and maybe nothing at any time. But you'd better lie low. You might be unduly suspected of ha'nting your own house!"

To the surprise of all present, Stebbins turned a chalky white, and whimpered a little, as he said, "I don't know what you mean,—I ain't done anything."

"See's you don't!" advised Crawford, enigmatically, and then the two doctors started to go on their second gruesome errand.

"This door's locked," announced Doctor Wayburn, trying to gain entrance to the Room with the Tassels.

"I have the key," said Eve Carnforth, slowly, and, with a white face, she offered it to the men.

"What are you doing with it?" asked Landon, in amazement.

"I d—don't know," and Eve showed great nervousness. "I think I feared some one would go in there."

The others looked at her curiously, for the white face was pallid and the scarlet line of her lips was thin and straight.

An exclamation from Doctor Wayburn claimed their attention, and speaking from the doorway of the Room with the Tassels, he said:

"There is no body here."

"What!" cried several at once, and crowded to the door.

"Absolutely none," repeated the doctor, and Professor Hardwick pushed his way past the two medical men and entered the room.

"It's gone!" he said, reappearing, "Vernie's body is gone!"

"Impossible!" cried Landon, "what do you mean? Why, we've all been right here all the morning! How could it be gone?"

"See for yourself," and Hardwick stepped aside. There was no denying the fact. Scrutiny of the whole room showed no presence of the cold, still form that had been reverently laid on that bed. Everybody entered and peered around, fruitlessly. They shook the heavy hangings and looked behind them, but to no avail.

Vernie's body had utterly disappeared!

CHAPTER 10: WAS IT SUPERNATURAL?

LATE that afternoon Braye returned from New York. He looked weary and exhausted, as if under hard and continuous strain.

Norma and Eve had both been watching for him from different windows and met on the stairs in their sudden rush to meet him in the hall.

It was easily apparent that both girls desired to see him first and tell him the further awful development of the disappearance of Vernie's body.

"What!" he exclaimed, "more horrors! Wait a minute, till I get off this dust coat."

Before Eve or Norma could say more, the others, hearing Braye, came trooping to the hall, and all began to talk at once.

"I can't understand" and Braye wearily passed his hand across his brow,—"tell me all that happened after I left last evening."

"Nothing especial," said Tracy, quietly. "We all went to bed early, at least, we went to our rooms. Professor Hardwick and I sat up half the night, talking. But we left Thorpe on guard in the hall here, and of course, it never occurred to any of us there was need of further precaution."

"Nor was there," said Eve, fixing her great eyes on Braye. "Nobody could possibly come in from outside and take that child away. The house is too securely locked for that, as we all know."

"Why should any one want to?" queried Braye, his face blank with amazement.

"No one did want to,—no one did do it," returned Eve. "You must admit, Rudolph, that the whole thing is supernatural,—that—"

"No, Eve, I can't do that." Braye spoke positively. "When I'm up here with you psychists, and in this atmosphere of mystery,—and Lord knows 'Black Aspens' is mysterious!—I get swayed over toward spiritualism, but when I go down to the city and talk with rational, hard headed men, I realize there's nothing in this poppycock!"

"Oh, you do!" and Eve's penetrating glance seemed to bore into his very soul, "then, pray, how do you explain the fact that Vernie—isn't there?"

"I don't know, Eve,—I don't know. But some fiend in human shape must have managed to get into the house-"

"And get out again?" said Tracy, "and carry the body with him,—when Thorpe sat right here in the hall—"

"Where was Thorpe?" asked Braye, suddenly.

"In a chair there, by that table," and Eve indicated a position well back in the great hall.

"Then he couldn't see the doors of both rooms" began Braye, but Professor Hardwick interrupted: "Nonsense, man, both doors were open, if any move had been made, Thorpe must have heard it."

"Both doors open," said Braye, "Norma, you said they were closed when you came down to breakfast."

"I asked Thorpe about that," said Tracy. "He told me that at daybreak, or soon after, he closed the doors, without looking in the rooms. He was scared, I think, though he won't admit that. He says, he thought the ladies would be coming down and the doors better be closed."

"That's all right, but it's strange that he didn't glance into the rooms."

"I don't think so," said Landon. "Thorpe was in charge, but he had no reason to think there had been any disturbance, and he is pretty well scared up over the whole matter. And I don't wonder."

"Nor I," said Braye. "It's all inexplicable. What's Crawford going to do next?"

"I'm not sure," said Tracy, "but I think he'll hold an inquest. Of course, he thinks it's a case of murder—"

"How absurd!" cried Eve. "What more does the man want in confirmation of the supernatural? First, those two deaths, impossible of human achievement, and now, the taking away of poor little Vernie, in circumstances that deny any mortal hand in the matter!"

"If that's true, Eve," Braye spoke in a matter of fact tone, "it will do no harm to let the coroner proceed along his own lines. He can't convict a murderer if there is one,—and if there is one, we all want him convicted, don't we?"

"Of course," said Landon, "but suppose they pitch on an innocent man?"

"It's all supposition," declared Braye. "I never heard of such a moil! I can't see how it can be murder, or body snatching, yet I can't stand for ghost work, either. Say it's murder,—where's a motive, for anybody?"

"I think you ought to know, Rudolph," Eve said, slowly, "that that Crawford person asked who would inherit Mr. Bruce's money, and—"

"And we owned up that you were the next of kin, old chap," put in Landon, smiling grimly. "Any remarks?"

"Don't be flippant, Wynne," said Braye, seriously, "of course, I've thought of that. I can't very well be charged with the murder, as I wasn't here at the time, but I do feel deeply embarrassed at the thought that I am, without a doubt, the next heir. That can, I suppose, draw suspicion on me, as I may be said to have motive. But I am not afraid of that, for there's no possible way I could have turned the trick. But, if it was murder, if there's the slightest indication of foul play, I'm ready to devote all of Uncle Gifford's money, if need be, in bringing the criminal to justice."

"Of course, there's no sense in tacking the crime on you, Braye," and Landon sighed. "If it was a crime, and if anybody here committed it, they'll more likely suspect me, for I'm the next heir after you, and if I could despatch two intervening heirs, I could also bump you off, I suppose."

"Don't talk like that, Wynne," implored Milly. "It's not like you, and I—"

"I'm only preparing you, Milly, dear, for what may come. That mutton headed coroner can't rest till he fastens murder on somebody,—and it might as well be me."

"I want to go home, Wynne,—I want to go back to New York," and Milly began to cry.

"You may, dear, just as soon as you like. But I must stay and see what happens up here. For me to run away would be, to say the least, suspicious."

"Talk sense, Wynne," broke in Braye; "I wasn't here, you know, when those two people died. Tell me again, just where were you all?"

"Mr. Bruce and Professor Hardwick sat in those two chairs, confabbing," Wynne explained; "I was passing things round, so was Mr. Tracy. Eve was running the tea things, Vernie was jumping about here and there, and Norma,—where were you, Norma?"

"I was near Mr. Bruce and the Professor, listening to their talk," she returned. "I was greatly interested. Mr. Landon had just given me a cup of tea, and I was sipping it as I listened. There was nothing wrong about the tea, of that I'm certain."

"Of course there wasn't," agreed Braye, who had heard the scene rehearsed many times. "There's nothing wrong anywhere, that I can see, except that a dreadful thing has happened, and we must find out all we can about it. I've been to see Uncle Gif's business friends, he has a few in New York, and they're flabbergasted, of course. One of them, a Mr. Jennings, is sure it's a desperate murder, cleverly contrived by some people in Chicago, who are enemies of Uncle's, and who, he says, are diabolically ingenious enough to have brought it about. He holds that Vernie's death was accidental,—I mean that they only intended to kill Uncle Gifford. I can't believe in this talk, for how could it have been brought about? But Jennings thinks it was through the servants,—and that they're really enemies in disguise."

"Why, they're all natives of this section," exclaimed the Professor, "how could they be implicated?"

"I told Jennings that, but he thinks they've been bought over, or—oh, Lord, I don't know *what* he thinks! I don't know what to think myself! There's *no* solution!"

"Don't think now, Rudolph," and Eve came over to his side, and took his hand in hers. "You're all tired out, and I don't wonder. Let's have tea,—we mustn't dread tea because of its associations,—if we do that, we'll all collapse."

With a determined air, Eve went away to order tea served as usual, though Milly had declared she never wanted to have it in that hall again.

But Eve's idea found favour with the rest, and they gratefully accepted the refreshment, which, until that awful afternoon, had been such a pleasant function.

"We must settle some things," Braye said, looking at Landon. "I arranged to send the bodies to Chicago,—of course, I didn't know—"

"Isn't it terrible!" exclaimed Norma. "What shall you do now?"

"I think I'll send Uncle Gif's body, at once, and hope to find Vernie's later. It *must* be found—" Braye looked about wildly. "I wish I had been here last night! Oh, forgive me, I'm not casting any hint of blame on you others, but,—well, you know I wasn't here when—when it happened, either, and I can't sense it all as you do. Professor Hardwick, what do you think about it all?"

"I'm an old man, Braye, and I've had wide experience, also, I'm a hard one to convince without strong and definite proof, but I'll state now, once for all, that I'm a complete convert to spiritism and I believe,—I know,— these deaths of our friends were the acts of an inimical spirit, a phantasm, incensed at our curiosity concerning the occult, and our frivolous attitude toward the whole subject."

"You really believe that, Professor?"

"I really do, Braye, and moreover I am convinced that the disappearance of—of little Vernie, is the work of the evil spirit. What else can explain it?"

"Nothing that I know of, but I can't swallow the idea of a disembodied spirit making off with a real, material body! I *wish* I'd been here! Didn't *anybody* see or hear *anything?*"

"No," declared Landon, but Norma gave a quick glance at Eve, who returned it with a defiant toss of her Titian coloured head.

"Why do you look at me like that, Norma?" she asked, shortly.

"Why do I?" Norma repeated in a soft significant tone. "I think you know, Eve."

"Well, I for one, shall stay up here for a time, and see how matters go on," said Braye, with sudden determination. "Who else wants to stay?"

"I do," said Professor Hardwick, "I think we've by no means seen the last of the manifestations, and though I feel there is a danger, I am ready to brave it for the sake of investigating further."

"I don't want to stay," and Milly shook with nervous apprehension. "Can't we go home, Wynne?"

"Very soon, darling. You can go at once, and I'll follow as soon as things are adjusted up here. I think none of us ought to seem to run away."

"Certainly not," Tracy agreed, promptly. "The whole affair is so astounding, I can scarcely get my wits together, but I see clearly, no one must leave this house, until we are all exonerated from suspicion."

"Not even me?" asked Milly, tearfully.

"That's for you and Mr. Landon to decide," returned Tracy, gently. "I'm not dictating, not even advising, but I have strong opinions on the subject. What say, Braye?"

"I quite agree with you, Tracy. But, I'm sure if Mrs. Landon prefers to go down to New York and stay at her mother's no one could possibly object."

"But I don't!" Milly surprised them all by saying, "if you put it that way,—if it's cowardly to go away, I don't want to go. I want to stay, if Wynne does, and if Eve and Norma stay."

"That's my brave girl," and Landon smiled at his wife; "I'll guarantee that Milly won't make any trouble, either. Once she's awake to a duty, she's bold as a lion. Now, see here, if Crawford stirs up suspicion of any of us, we'll have to deal with him pretty roughly, I fear. He's a pig headed sort, and he will move heaven and earth to gain his point. Moreover, we can't expect him to subscribe to spook theories, any more than those men Rudolph talked to in New York. One has to go through some such experiences as we have, to believe in them. You, Professor, would never have been convinced by hearsay evidence, would you?"

"No, sir, I would not! It took these otherwise inexplicable happenings to prove to me that there is but one way to look. Even a coroner can't produce a human criminal who could kill those two people the way they were killed, and who could get into and out of this house and take a human body with him! The thing is preposterous!"

"You know the doors and windows were all locked?" asked Braye, thoughtfully.

"I looked after them, myself," said Landon. "I always do. After the last one goes upstairs for the night, I invariably look after the locking up. And the house, properly locked, is impregnable. The servants' quarters are shut off and locked; there is absolutely no way of getting in from outside."

"Going back to Jennings' theory," mused Braye, "could we suspect old Thorpe?"

"Not for a minute," declared Landon. "And, too, he wasn't in the hall when they died. No, I'd trust Thorpe as far as I would any of ourselves. But, there's Stebbins. I've never felt sure that he's entirely trustworthy."

"Even so," said Braye, "he wasn't here when—when they died."

"No, he wasn't. I can't see any way he could have arranged things unless he poisoned the cake—"

"Rubbish, Wynne!" cried Eve, "you know we all ate that cake. Do be rational."

"But Mr. Bruce was poisoned, Eve, we can't get away from that."

"Of course he was," broke in Hardwick, "and doubtless Vernie was too, but it was not done by human agency."

"Well, there we go, reasoning round in a circle," murmured Norma; "I think our talk is useless, when we surmise and speculate about it all. Let us decide on our immediate plans. Shall you send Mr. Bruce's body to Chicago, and stay here yourself, Rudolph?"

"Yes, as I look at it now. I can't see anything else to do."

Nor was there anything else to do.

For Doctor Crawford persisted in treating the case as a criminal one, and requested that all concerned remain at Black Aspens for the present, with a hint that unless they did so, the request might become a command.

"Then you think the two people were murdered?" asked Landon of the county physician.

"I don't say that, for sure; but when a man drops dead, and a trace of poison is found in his stomach, it looks mighty like an intention of death on some one's part,— maybe the man himself. There's a show of suicide, you know."

"But Gifford Bruce never would commit suicide!"

"If only those committed suicide who are expected to do so, there'd be mighty few of them. Now, I hold that poison was taken into Mr. Bruce's stomach while he was eating that cake, or whatever he did eat."

"We agree to that," Landon spoke slowly, "but some of us think the poison was put in by supernatural means."

"Now, ain't that nonsense,—for reasonable, rational men!" and Crawford's fine scorn nettled Landon.

"Professor Hardwick doesn't think it nonsense," he returned.

The two were alone, Crawford having asked an interview with the man who had rented the house.

"Professor!" and Crawford fairly snorted. "For fool theories, commend me to a college professor. They can't see two inches either side of their noses!"

"We have had reason to believe in spiritual manifestations," went on Braye.

"Yes, and who gave you those reasons? Who rented this house to you folks, for the sole purpose of supplying you with a ha'nted house! Who knew that ghosts must be forthcoming, if you folks was to be satisfied? Who performed ghost doings himself, in order that you might not be disappointed?"

"What are you implying? That Mr.—that the owner tricked us?"

"That's for you to find out. You came up here to investigate, as I understand it. Well, why don't you investigate? You swallow all them ghosts and ha'ntings, and never look around to see who's fooling you!"

"But, Doctor Crawford, what you insinuate is not possible. All the strange things we have seen or heard have occurred at night, or,—yes,—occasionally in the daytime, but always when Mr. Stebbins was at his home in East Dryden."

"How do you know he was?"

"Why, he has never been to the house at all, except two or three times on commonplace errands, since we've been here. The supernatural manifestations we have observed had no more to do with him than they had with you!"

"That's as may be. Only I advise you to investigate with a little common sense and not too much blind faith in your spook visitors. Now, Mr. Landon, I take it you're boss around here."

"I'm responsible for the house rent, if that's what you mean."

"Well, that'll do. Now, sir, there's got to be an inquest. I expected, of course, to hold it on the two bodies, but since one's gone, we'll have to do what we can without it. I don't deny that this case is beyond all my experience. I've sent for a detective from New York, and I'll get all the other help I need. But I'm all at sea, myself, and I make no secret of that."

"I thought you suspected Eli Stebbins."

"Not of murder! No, sir! Me'n Eli, we ain't good friends, haven't been for years, and I wouldn't put it past him to play ghost to scare you city people, but murder! Land, no, I wouldn't ever accuse Eli Stebbins of goin' that far!"

"Have you any definite suspect?"

"I don't say as I have, and I don't say as I ain't. Truth is, I'm all afloat. I don't know which way to turn. Every thing's so awful unbelievable,—as you might say. Now, there's them two Thorpes. Good, steady going New England people, they are, and yet, if I had any reason to suspect 'em, I can see myself doing so. But, land, there ain't a shred of evidence that way. Why, they wasn't even in the room when the two of 'em died!"

"Wait a minute, Doctor Crawford. Nobody was in the room at the time of those two deaths, but our own party. You don't suspect one of us, do you?"

"No, Mr. Landon, I don't. You ain't a gay crowd, nor yet a fast or a common crowd. You're all high toned, quiet, law abiding citizens,—as I size you up. To be sure, decent citizens have committed murder, but I can't connect up any one of you with crime in this case. I know Mr. Braye will inherit the money that old Mr. Bruce left, and I know that you're related there, too, but I haven't seen one iota of reason to suspect any one of your crowd. If I do, I'll let you know mighty quick! Nor can I hang it on the Thorpes; nor yet on those girls they have in to help. And that's what the inquest's for. To bring out, if possible, some evidence against somebody, so's we can get a start."

"I fear you can't get that evidence, Doctor, for if there were any we would have found it ourselves. You have my good wishes, for if it is a case of murder, committed by a living, human villain, we most assuredly want him apprehended."

"He will be, Mr. Landon, take it from me, he will be!"

Chapter 11: The Heir Speaks Out

THE days that followed were like an awful nightmare to the people most interested. But at last the inquest was over, the body of Gifford Bruce had been sent to Chicago for burial, and a strange quiet had settled down upon the household at Black Aspens.

No new facts had transpired at the inquest. Though the police tried hard to fasten the crime on some individual, there was no definite evidence against any one. All those who had been present at the mysterious death hour told their stories straightforwardly and unshakably. All agreed as to the circumstances, all remembered and related the story of the Ouija board, which foretold the death of two of the party at four o'clock.

"Who was pushing that board?" the coroner asked.

"Miss Reid and myself," Tracy spoke up. "We had been playing with it for some time, and having had only uninteresting and trifling results we were about to lay the thing aside, when the message came that two of us would die the next day at four o'clock. Miss Reid seemed frightened, but I thought at the time she had spelled out the message, herself, to get up a little excitement. However, I took the board away from her at once, feeling that she was carrying a jest too far. I think now, that she was innocent in the matter—"

"Well, I don't," said the coroner. "If that girl made up that message, she had a reason. Probably she was responsible for both deaths."

"Impossible!" cried Tracy, shocked at this theory. "Why, she was but a child, she had no thought of suicide or—or murder! If she faked the message, it was merely in fun, and because she had tried all evening to get some message of interest. It is quite possible she made up the message, but it is not possible that she did it otherwise than as a jest."

"A gruesome jest!"

"As it turned out, yes, indeed. But either it was in jest,—or—the message was from a supernatural source."

Tracy's eyes were deeply sorrowful, and his face expressed a sort of awed wonder that made many who were present think that after all there might be something in these occult beliefs.

But not so the coroner. He refused to consider the Ouija message with any serious interest, and continued to ply his witnesses with questions both pertinent and wide of the mark.

Elijah Stebbins was put through a grilling inquiry. His manner was that of a guilty man, but no proof of crime could be found in connection with him. The day and hour of the two deaths, he was proved to have been at his home in East Dryden, beyond all doubt. Even granting that the Thorpes, one or both, were in his employ, there was no reason to suspect them. If they had put poison in the cakes or in the tea, it must have been done in the kitchen, and therefore would have affected the whole supply. Suspicion must fall, if anywhere, on the members of the house party who were present at the hour of four o'clock on the fatal day.

But these, as has been said, gave so clear a statement of the actual happenings at that hour, that there was no loophole for suspicion to enter. Moreover, the fact that the deaths occurred simultaneously, and just at the foretold hour, seemed to preclude all possibility of any human means being employed. It did look like a supernatural occurrence and many who would have scorned such a belief, were inevitably led to agree that no other theory could explain it.

Yet the coroner and his jury were unwilling to admit this, and the verdict was the one most frequently heard of, murder by a person or persons unknown.

Indeed, what else could it have been? A coroner's jury can't accuse a nameless ghost of two murders, by poison. They pinned their faith to that poison, discovered in the stomach of the body of Gifford Bruce. They assumed that Miss Reid died from the effects of the same poison, but how administered or by whom, or what had become of the body of Miss Reid, they had no idea. But of one thing they were sure, that all these things, and all parts of the complicated crime, were the work of human hands and human intelligence, and that for the reputation of their village and their county and their state, the murderer must be discovered and brought to justice.

But how? How find a criminal who gave no signs of existence, and who was, by those most closely concerned, denied actual existence?

The detective, one Dan Peterson, proceeded on the theory that a closed mouth implies great secret wisdom. He said little, save to ask questions of everybody with whom he came in contact, and as these questions merely carried him round in a circle back to his starting point, he made little progress.

There were also, of course, many reporters, from the city papers, and these wrote up the story as their natures or their chiefs dictated. Some played up the supernatural side for all it was worth, and more; others scorned such foolishness, and treated the affair as a desperate and unusually mysterious murder case. But all agreed that it was the most sensational and interesting affair of its sort that had happened in years, and the eager reporters hung around and nearly drove frantic the feminine members of the house party.

At last, Norma and Milly refused to see them, but Eve Carnforth continued to talk with them, and imbued many of them, more or less, with her occult views.

"There's something in what that red headed woman says," one reporter opined to his fellow.

"She puts it mighty convincing,—if you ask me."

"Yes, and why?" jeered his friend, "because she's the man behind the ghost!"

"What! Miss Carnforth! Guilty? Never!"

"I'm not so sure. You know as well as I do, that spook talk is all rubbish, but she's so bent and determined to stuff it down everybody's neck, I think she's hiding her own hand in the matter."

"You do! Well, you'd better think again, before you let out any such yarn as that! Why, she's a queen, that woman is!"

"Oho! She's subjugated you, has she? Well, look out that she doesn't convert you to spookism,—you'd lose your job!"

Other curious people journeyed up to Black Aspens for the pleasure of looking at the house where the mystery was staged. If allowed to enter they walked about, open mouthed in admiration or wonder.

"Stunning hall!" exclaimed one young man, a budding architect, who examined the old house with interest. "Look at those bronze columns! I never saw such a pair."

"I've heard the first Montgomery brought those from Italy or somewhere, and put up a house behind 'em," volunteered another sightseer. "Ain't it queer, the way they're half in and half out of the front wall? Land! You wouldn't know whether you was going to school or coming home!" and the speaker laughed heartily at his own wit.

But at last, the sightseers were refused admittance to the house, and the remaining members of the party gathered in conclave to decide on future plans.

Professor Hardwick was the one who showed the calmest demeanour.

"If there was a chance of a human being having committed these crimes," he said, "I'd be the first one to want to track him down, and send him straight to the chair. But nobody who has thought about the matter can present any theory that will account for the human element in the cause of the tragedy. Therefore, feeling certain, as I do, that our friends were killed by supernatural influences, I am ready to stay here a short time longer, in hopes of convincing the authorities up here that we are right. Moreover, I planned to stay here a month, and we've been here but little more than a fortnight."

"I'm willing to stay for the same reason, Professor," and Eve Carnforth's strange eyes glowed deeply. "I too, know that no living beings brought about the deaths of Mr. Bruce and little Vernie, and I will stay the rest of our proposed month, if the others will."

"I am ready to stay," said Milly Landon, quietly. "I've gotten all over my hysterical, foolish fears, and I want to stay. I have a good reason, and if I hadn't, I'd be willing to stay to keep house for the rest of you."

"Let's consider it settled, then," said Landon, "that we stay a couple of weeks longer. The astute detective, Mr. Peterson, thinks he can round up the villains who did the awful things, and if he can, I'm ready to appear against them."

"We're all ready to do that," agreed Mr. Tracy, "and I'll stay a week or so, but I want to get away by the middle of August."

"That's nearly two weeks hence," observed Norma, "I'd like to go home about that time, too. And all that's to be discovered, which, I suppose, will be nothing, ought to be found out in that time."

"It wouldn't surprise me to have some further spiritual manifestations," the Professor stated, with a deeply thoughtful air. "I don't know why there wouldn't be such."

"Not with fatal results, I hope," and Mr. Tracy shuddered.

"I hope not, too," and the Professor looked grave. "But if we receive another warning, I shall go home at once."

"I don't think we will," Eve said, "I think there was a reason for the wrath of the phantasms, and now that wrath is appeased. We must not provoke it further."

"You know," Norma added, "the two who—who died, were scoffers at the idea of spiritual visitations."

"Uncle Gif was," said Braye, "but little Vernie wasn't."

"Oh, yes, she was," corrected Eve. "She made fun of our beliefs all along. And if she really made the Ouija write that message in a spirit of bravado, it's small wonder that the vengeance reached her as well as Mr. Bruce, who openly jeered at it all."

"I can't think it," mused Tracy, "that sweet, lovable child,—full of mischief, of course, but simple, harmless mischief,—"

"But, Mr. Tracy," Norma looked and spoke positively, "it's easier to think of a supernatural spirit wanting to harm the child, than a living person! What possible cause could a human being have to wish harm to little Vernie Reid?"

"That's true, Miss Cameron. But it's inexplicable, however you look at it."

"At the same time," Braye argued, "we must give both sides a chance. If there is any trick or scheme that a man might have used to bring about those deaths at that moment,—I can't conceive of any, but if there should have been such,—we must, of course, give all possible assistance to Mr. Peterson in his search."

"I'm more than willing," said Tracy, "I'm anxious to help him for, as you say, Braye, if there's a human mind capable of devising means to commit such a crime, it surely ought to be within the province of some other human mind to discover it."

"Suppose we start out on that basis," suggested Braye. "I mean, assume that a live person did the deed, and it's up to us to find him. Then if we can't do it, fall back on our occult theories."

"I know where I'd look first," said Landon, grimly.

"Where?"

"Toward Eli Stebbins. I've always thought he or the Thorpes, or all of them together, know more than we suspect they do. Why, think a minute. Do you remember the first queer, inexplicable thing that happened up here?"

"I do," Eve spoke up. "It was the night we arrived. That battered old candlestick moved itself from Mr. Bruce's room to Vernie's."

"Yes, Eve, that's what I have in mind. Well, I thought then, and I think now, that Stebbins moved that thing himself."

"Why?" asked several voices at once.

"I thought I saw him sneaking across the hall that night. And as you know, none of us would have done it, and I don't think Mr. Bruce did. I thought that at first, but since Mr. Bruce's death, I know he never played any tricks on us."

"Oh, that doesn't follow," objected Hardwick. "I always suspected Bruce would trick us if he could, but when it came to his own death, I've no notion that he compassed that!"

"No," agreed Braye, "whatever the truth may be, there was no suicide."

And so they talked, discussed, surmised, argued and theorized, without getting any nearer a positive belief, or proof of any sort to uphold their opinions.

Each seemed to have marked out a certain line of thought and doggedly stuck to it.

Professor Hardwick was, perhaps, the one most positive regarding supernatural causes, though Eve and Norma were almost equally certain.

Braye and Landon were not entirely willing to accept these beliefs, but confessed they had no plausible substitutes to suggest. Tracy, as a clergyman, was loth to accept what seemed to him heathen ideas, but he was more or less influenced by the talk of the Professor and of Eve Carnforth, who was exceedingly persuasive in manner and argument.

Milly had little thought of her own about the matter, but was always ready to believe as her husband did, though, she, too, was swayed by the strong statements and declarations of Eve Carnforth.

But Dan Peterson paid no more heed to ghost lore of any sort or kind than as if the words had not been spoken. Miss Carnforth's glib recital of wonders she knew to be true, Miss Cameron's quiet statements that she vouched for as facts, the Professor's irascible arguments, all were as nothing to the practical, hard headed detective.

"No, ma'am," he said to Eve; "it ain't that I doubt your word, but those things don't go down. I've seen criminals before, try to get out by blaming ghosts, but they couldn't put it over."

"Are you implying that one of us may be guilty!" cried Eve, really incensed at the thought.

"I'm not implying anything, ma'am. I'm investigating. When I find out anything, I'll accuse, I won't imply."

The man's personality was not unpleasant. Of a commonplace type, he went about his business cheerfully, and in a practical, common sense fashion. He examined the great hall, where the deaths had occurred, for a possible secret entrance.

"Nothing doing," was his sum up of this investigation. "That mahogany wall of the vestibule is as solid as a rock, and nobody could get through those bronze doors when they're locked and fastened with those bolts!"

"Are you assuming that some one entered and killed the victims, as we all sat round drinking tea?" exclaimed the Professor, irascibly.

"Not just that, sir," returned Peterson, gravely. "But somebody might have entered in the night, say, and secreted himself,—"

"And then appeared to poison the cake when we weren't looking!" jeered Landon.

"Well," and the detective looked a little sheepish, "I got to consider all points, you know. And there don't seem to be any clues—of any sort."

"No," said Braye, "no dropped handkerchief or broken cuff link. Those would be a help, wouldn't they?"

"And then," Landon went on, "usually, there's somebody who had a quarrel with the victim, and so, can be duly suspected. But there's nothing of that sort in this case."

"Nobody at odds with Mr. Bruce, wasn't there?" asked the detective, hopefully.

"Nobody," declared Landon. "Now you may as well know all there is to know, Peterson. Mr. Braye here, is the heir to Mr. Bruce's large fortune. After him, I inherit. If these facts are of the nature of straws to show you which way the wind blows, make the most of them. But do it openly. If you suspect Mr. Braye or myself, even in the slightest degree, tell us so. Don't work behind our backs. We're ready and willing to help you. That's so, Braye?"

"Rather, Wynne! Moreover, if there's any way to use it, the fortune of Uncle Bruce is at the disposal of anybody who can bring the criminal to justice. I don't want the money,—at least, I can't enjoy it, and don't want it, considering the way it has come to me. I shall endow a hospital or something with it. For, truly,—I may be foolish, but I can't seem to see myself living luxuriously on money that has come to me as this has. I don't wonder that to an outsider, it might look very much as if I had removed these two people in order that I might acquire riches, or, it would have looked so, if I had been here at the time. I doubt if the most fertile imagination can invent a way I could have been the criminal when I was in East Dryden shopping with Mrs. Landon."

"Also, Mr. Peterson," Landon resumed, "remember that I am the next to inherit, and if I could have compassed the taking off of these two, I could doubtless have later despatched Mr. Braye, and so have come into the fortune myself."

"Wynne," pleaded Milly, "*don't* say those things! They're too absurd!"

"Not that, Milly dear. Mr. Peterson might easily take up some such line of deduction, and while I'm willing he should do so, and proceed in any way he chooses, I repeat that I want him to do it openly, and not try to convict Rudolph or myself, behind our backs. When I proffer him my help, it is in a real and sincere offer of assistance, and I want him to be equally frank and outspoken."

"I guess you're pretty safe in your attitude," said Peterson, smiling. "Criminals don't speak right out in meeting, like that. And I don't suspect you gentlemen, if you *are* heirs to the property. I think there's others to be suspected, and I promise you, sir, if I'm led toward any of your party here, I'll tell you what I'm up to."

"That's enough, Peterson, I trust you to keep your word, and you may rely on us to help in any way we can."

And so life at Black Aspens settled down to its former routine, at least in matters of daily household affairs. But the actuating principle of the psychic investigators had changed. Those who thoroughly believed in occultism, sought expectantly for further proofs. Those who were still uncertain, awaited developments. And those who had little or no belief in the supernatural sought some clues or hints that might point to a human criminal.

Dan Peterson was among these last. A good, able minded detective, though not of the transcendental type found in story books, he worked diligently at his problem, which seemed to him a harder one than he had ever before tackled.

His suspicions were all toward the servants of the house, and with these he included Elijah Stebbins.

Nor was he illogical in his thoughts. Stebbins was acting queerly. He was frightened at questions, and was difficult to get hold of for an interview. He answered at random, frequently contradicted himself, and showed a positive terror of his own house, since the tragedies there.

"If he killed those two people with his own hands, he couldn't act any different," Peterson said to Landon, whom he frequently consulted. "But I can't imagine any way to connect him up with it. He was home in East Dryden when they died, and that's certain. Now, if he could have made old Thorpe act as his tool—but, Lord, why would he do it, anyhow! It's too absurd to think Stebbins would want to take those two lives! He wanted you people should be scared, that I'm sure of. He did all he could to scare you,—that I know. But as to killing any of you, I'm sure he didn't. Howsumever, somebody committed those murders, and I'm going to find out who!"

CHAPTER 12: THE PROFESSOR'S EXPERIENCE

BUT the days passed by, and Dan Peterson was unable to make good his word. Everybody, outside of the immediate household at Black Aspens believed the two mysterious deaths were the result of the murderous intent of one or more human beings, and refused absolutely to consider the spook nonsense offered in explanation by the friends and relatives of the victims.

Meanwhile there were a few further inexplicable happenings in the old house. Now and then, one or another would notice the odour of prussic acid, or would report a glimpse of a ghostly figure prowling round at night, or tell of hearing low moans at four o'clock in the morning.

But, usually, these were the experiences of only one, and lacking corroboration, could be set down to imagination, which was now especially vivid in all the party. Often Eve or Norma recounted some of these mysteries, but Landon laughed at them and said the girls had been dreaming.

Professor Hardvvick experienced no similar illusions, though he longed to do so. Indeed, he really watched and listened, hoping for some message or manifestation from his friend, Gifford Bruce. But none was vouchsafed to him, and though interested in the experiences of the others, he still longed for a personal experience. And finally one came to him.

At four o'clock one morning, he lay awake, as often, listening to the strokes of the hall clock, which none of them could ever hear without a thrill, and slowly in at his bedroom door floated a dim, ghostly shape.

There was not sufficient light for him to discern more than the outline of what seemed to be a tall, gaunt figure, with a shawl over its head. Nearer to him the thing came, and the old Professor felt himself grow cold with fear. He had often boasted of his desire to see the ghost, and of his scorn of fear in connection therewith. But now, that the spectre had really appeared to him, the old man trembled all over, and tried in vain to cry out.

His throat contracted, his tongue was powerless, and a sort of paralysis of terror held him in thrall.

The approaching figure seemed not to walk, but progressed by a strange gliding motion, and came within a foot or two of the bed, where the Professor lay, shivering with dread.

Still but a misty wraith, the awful thing leaned over the prostrate man and as the shawled head drew near, Professor Hardwick saw dimly the face of his visitor, and it was a skull!

The fearsome sight of hollow eye sockets and grinning, fleshless jaws, gave a sudden strength to the frightened man, and he uttered a faint terrorized scream.

Slowly the spectre raised a long, white draped arm, and Hardwick saw a small glass tumbler in front of his face. Only for an instant, and then the phantom faded away, and vanished into space.

Again the Professor called out, and hurrying footsteps were heard in the hall.

Mr. Tracy was away in Boston, and Rudolph Braye had gone to New York, so the only other man in the house was Landon, who came hastily to the Professor's door in his dressing gown and slippers.

"What is it," he asked, "did you call? Are you ill?"

"The—the ghost—" the old man articulated with difficulty.

"Nonsense!" said Landon, "you've been dreaming. Where's a ghost? I just came along the corridor, and I didn't see any."

"Don't tell me I didn't see it," babbled the Professor. "I did, Wynne, as plain as I see you now."

Landon had brought his own bedroom candle, and by its scant light he scanned the old man's face.

"You're all scared up, Professor," he said, kindly. "Guess I'll give you a nightcap, and send you back to sleep again, it's only four or so."

"I know it, Wynne, it was just four when that—that thing came. I wasn't asleep, I haven't been for an hour or more. Just at four o'clock,—the hall clock was striking,—I saw that awful thing come stalking in—and—and it had a death's head under that white shawl—"

"Hold on, there, Professor, if that's so, there must be somebody who did the stalking! I'm going to make search."

Landon called Thorpe, and together the two went over the whole house, searching in every nook and cranny that could possibly conceal an intruder. But none was found. Every door and window was securely fastened, and as Landon had often observed, not a mouse could get into Black Aspens, once it was locked up for the night.

"Nothing doing, Professor," he reported cheerfully, after the search. "We lighted up the whole place, and we scoured for burglars or ghost pretenders, but nothing human has entered this house to night. Nor was your spook any of ourselves, for Milly has rounded up the girls, and I've made sure that the doors that shut off the servants' quarters have not been opened. Now, what have you to say?"

"Only that I saw the thing," the Professor had pulled himself together, "and I'm not prepared to say whether I think it was a phantom or a person pretending to be one. You're sure about the servants?"

"Absolutely, they couldn't get through."

"What about Stebbins? Could he have been concealed in the house all night?"

"No; and if he had, how could he have got out? All the doors and windows are locked on the inside, just as they've been all night. He couldn't lock them behind him."

"Thorpe could let him in and out, if he wanted to."

"Into the back part of the house. But Thorpe himself can't get into the main house, the rooms that we use, after I lock the doors between. Come, now, Professor, you know all that as well as I do. Either you dreamed your ghost, or it's the real thing, this time. Take your choice."

Landon was so cheerful and took the thing so lightly, that Hardwick began to feel more at ease, and recounted his story in further detail. "It was the real thing," he concluded. "I wish Rudolph or Mr. Tracy had been here. They sleep in this wing, and they would have come to me more quickly than you did, Wynne."

"I came the moment I heard you call, at least, as soon as I could slip into a bathrobe."

"I know you did, and it wouldn't have mattered. That thing didn't walk away down the corridor, you know, it just faded away,—vanished into the air. I could see it—"

"How could you, with no light?"

"I don't know how I did. It wasn't exactly luminous, and yet it gave out a very faint glow, enough for me to see it, anyhow. Oh, I shall never forget its awful grin!"

Professor Hardwick told his tale to Eve and Norma later in the day, and in the afternoon the men returned. Mr. Tracy said he had been to Boston, to see the trustees of a church that had called him to its pastorate, and Braye had been in New York looking after some of his late uncle's business affairs.

Both men were deeply interested in the story of the ghost, for as they said, Professor Hardwick was not one to imagine or to think himself awake when he was dreaming.

They listened attentively, and Tracy summed it up by saying, "Well, if Professor Hardwick saw that, it makes me feel like believing in the supernatural."

"Me, too," agreed Braye. "I don't take much stock in the stories of the girls, for Eve is a visionary creature, and Norma is very imaginative. But when a rational, scientific man sees things, I believe the things are there to be seen! At least, I'm willing to believe. I would feel more certain if I saw it myself,—and yet,—to tell the truth I've no desire to see it. I'll take other people's words for it. How about you, Tracy?"

"I don't believe I'm psychic, or sensitive, or whatever you call it," and the clergyman smiled. "You know I slept in the Room with the Tassels, but no ghostly visitor favoured me."

"It may come to you yet," said Hardwick, turning grave eyes on Tracy, "or you, either, Rudolph. You see, it doesn't visit only that room. I wish some of you others could see it, I'd feel more sure of my own story."

"Aren't you sure of it?" asked Tracy.

"What do you mean by sure?" queried the Professor, a little petulantly. "Of course, I'm sure I saw what I've told you, but I want to be sure it was a ghost, and not a person tricking me. Could it have been Miss Carnforth, now?"

"No, it wasn't," declared Landon. "Milly went to the girls as I went to you, Professor, and found them both asleep. Or at least they were dozing, but they were safely in their beds. You know we're all more or less wakeful at four A.M."

"Four P.M. is a more fatal time," said Braye, musingly. "The whole thing is frightful. I'm for going back to New York, as soon as we can."

"If this should be the eleventh case," began the Professor.

"What do you mean, the eleventh case?"; asked Tracy.

"As I told these people before we started up here, Andrew Lang has said, in one of his books, that ten out of every eleven cases of so called supernatural manifestations are produced by fraud. When I said that, Miss Carnforth very astutely said, that it was the eleventh case that was of interest to investigators. And I agreed. If this, now, is the eleventh case,—I don't mean only my experience of last night, but all our experiences up here,—if this is the eleventh case, that is *not* the result of fraud, and it certainly looks like it, why, then, we have something worth investigating."

"Not at the cost of any more lives," said Braye, sternly. "If it is the eleventh case, and if it is going right on being an eleventh case, I've had enough of it! Perhaps that apparition of a glass in the spectre's hand, foretells tragedy to you, Professor."

Braye spoke gloomily, rather than as an alarmist, but the Professor turned white. "I've thought of that," he said, in a low voice. "That's why I want to be sure the phantom was a real one. If it was fraud, I have no fear, but if it was really the disembodied spirit of that shawled woman, appearing in her own materialized skeleton,—I, too, have had about enough investigating!"

"What do you think, Norma?" Braye asked of the girl, as, later in the afternoon, they were walking round along the wild path that was the only approach to the great portals of Black Aspens.

"I don't know, Rudolph, but I'm beginning to think there *is* a human hand and brain back of it all. I'm a sensitive, and that's one reason why these things *don't* appeal to me as supernatural. I've had more or less experience with supernormal matters and I've never known anything like the things that have happened and are happening up here."

"Whom do you suspect, Norma? Tell me, for I, too, think there may be some trickery, and I wonder if we look in the same direction."

"I don't want even to hint it, Rudolph, but—"

"Don't hesitate to tell me, dear. Oh, that slipped out! I've no right to say' dear ' to you, but, —Norma, after we get back to town, after these horrors are farther in the past, mayn't I tell you then,—what I hope you will be glad to hear?"

"Don't—don't say such things," and a pained look came into the blue eyes. "You know you are not free to talk like that!"

"Not free? Why am I not? What do you mean?"

"You know, you must know. Eve told me—"

"Eve couldn't have told you that there was anything between her and me! Why, Norma, I have loved you from the very first moment I laid eyes on you! I have kept myself from telling you, because of all these dreadful things that have been going on. This atmosphere is no place for lovemaking, but, dearest, just give me a gleam of hope that later,—when we go back home, that I may—"

"Oh, Rudolph! Look! What is that? See, in the Room with the Tassels!"

They had neared the house on their return stroll, and from the window of the fatal room peered out at them a ghastly, grinning skull!

It was nearly dusk, but they could see quite clearly the hollow eye sockets and the awful teeth of the fleshless face.

Norma clung to Braye, almost fainting. He slipped an arm round her saying, "Brace up, Norma, dearest, be brave. This is our chance. Let us dash right in, and see if it is still there. Stay here, if you prefer, but I must go!"

He hastened toward the house, and Norma kept pace with him. She felt imbued with his spirit of courage and bravery, and together they hurried and burst in at the front door, which was never locked save at night.

Without stopping, Braye rushed into the Room with the Tassels. But there was no one there, and no sign of any occupant, either human or supernatural.

There was no one in the hall, and further search showed no one in the drawing room. Nor could anything unusual be found in the house.

Most of the people were in their rooms. Eve was partly ill with a headache, and Milly was looking after her.

The men appeared as Braye and Norma called out, and soon all had gathered to hear the strange new story.

"I shouldn't believe it, if you hadn't both seen it," said the Professor, "but I can't think you were both under the spell of imagination."

"I want to go home," Milly said, plaintively, "I, don't want to see the thing, and I'm afraid I'll be the next one it will visit."

"We will go, dear," said Landon. "As soon as we can make arrangements we'll get off. Don't you say so, Eve?"

"Yes," she assented, but slowly. "I would prefer to stay a bit longer, myself, but I really don't think Milly ought to. However, I'll do as the majority wish."

But the matter of going away from Black Aspens was not entirely at their own disposal. The detective, Dan Peterson, had been exceedingly busy, and had wrung a confession out of Elijah Stebbins. It had been a mild sort of third degree, but it had resulted in a frank avowal of Stebbins' implication in some, at least, of the mysterious happenings that had puzzled the people at Black Aspens.

Stebbins defended himself by the statement that he only rented his house on the understanding that it was haunted. He said, it was reputed haunted, but he knew that unless something mysterious occurred, the tenants would feel dissatisfied.

He said, too, that he saw no harm in doing a few little tricks to mystify and interest the investigators, but he swore that he had no hand in the spectral appearances nor in the awful tragedy of the four o'clock tea.

What he did confess to was the placing of the old, battered candlestick in Miss Reid's room the first night the party arrived.

"I done it, sort of on impulse," he said; "I heard 'em talking about ghosts, and just to amaze them, I sneaked in in the night and took that candlestick off en Mr. Bruce's dresser and set it on the young lady's. I didn't mean any harm, only to stir things up."

"Which you did," remarked Peterson drily. "Go on."

The confession was being recorded in the presence of police officials, and Stebbins was practically under arrest, or would be very shortly after his tale was told.

"Well, then, the first night Mr. Bruce slept in that room, that ha'nted room, I thought I'd wrap a sheet round me and give him a little scare,—he was so scornful o' ghosts, you know. An' I did, but nobody would believe his yarn. So that's all I did. If any more of them ghost performances was cut up by live people, they wasn't me. Somebody else did it."

And no amount of further coercion could budge Stebbins from these statements. He stuck to it, that though he had tricked his tenants, he had done nothing to harm them, and his intentions were of the best, as he merely wanted to give them what they had taken his house for.

"You intended to keep it up?" asked Peterson.

"Yes, I did, but after they took things into their own hands, and played spooks themselves, what was the use?"

"How did you get into the house at night, when it was so securely locked?" asked Peterson.

"I managed it, but I won't tell you how," said Stebbins, doggedly.

"With Thorpe's help," suggested Peterson, "or—oh, by Jinks!" he whistled; "I think I begin to see a glimmer of a gleam of light on this mystery! Yes, I sure do! Excuse me, and I'll fly over to the house and do a little questioning. Officer, keep friend Stebbins safe against my return."

Arrived at Black Aspens, Peterson asked for Rudolph Braye, and was closeted with him for a secret session, from which Braye came forth looking greatly worried and perturbed.

Peterson went away, and Braye sought the others. He found them listening to a letter which Professor Hardwick had just received and which the old man was reading aloud.

"It's from Mr. Wise," he said to Braye, as the latter came in hearing. "He's a detective, and he writes to me, asking permission to take up this case."

"What a strange thing to do!" exclaimed Braye.

"Yes," agreed Hardwick, "and he seems to be a strange man. Listen; 'If I succeed in finding a true solution to the mystery, you may pay me whatever you deem the matter worth, if I do not, there will be no charge of any sort. Except that I should wish to live in the house with you all, at Black Aspens. I know all of the affair that has been printed in the newspapers, and no more. If you are still in the dark, I should like prodigiously to get into the thick of it and will arrive as soon as you summon me."

There was more to the letter but that was the gist of it, and Braye listened in silence.

"I think," he said, as the Professor finished, "that we don't want that detective poking into our affairs."

"I agree," said Landon. "There's been quite enough publicity about all this already, and I, for one, prefer to go back to New York and forget it as soon as we can."

"We can't forget it very soon, Wynne," put in Milly, "but I, too, want to go back to New York."

"We can't go right off," Braye told them, "we must wait a week or so, at least."

"Why?" asked Eve, not at all displeased by this statement, for she frankly admitted a desire to stay longer at Black Aspens.

"Oh, lots of reasons." Braye put her off. "But let's settle down for another week here, and then we'll see."

"Then I'm going to tell Wise to come up for that week," declared the Professor. "I don't altogether adhere to my conviction as to supernatural powers, and I want to see what a big, really clever detective can dig up in the way of clues or evidence or whatever they work by."

"Oh, cut out Wise," urged Braye. "We don't want any more detectives than we are ourselves. And Peterson is pretty busy just now, too."

It was after the confab broke up that Milly went to Braye.

"Why don't you want Mr. Wise to come?" she said, without preamble.

"Why, oh,—why just 'cause I don't," he stammered, in an embarrassed way.

"You can't fool me, Rudolph," she said, with an agonized look on her pretty face. "You are afraid he'll suspect Wynne,—aren't you?"

"Don't, Milly," urged Braye, "*don't* say such things!"

"You are! I know from the way you try to put me off. Oh, Braye, he *didn't* do it! He hadn't any hand in any of the queer doings, had he, Rudolph? Tell me you know he hadn't!"

"Of course, Milly, of course."

"But, listen, Rudolph, I heard some of the things that Peterson man said to you, I listened at the door, I couldn't help it."

"Milly! I'm ashamed of you!"

"I don't care! I'm not ashamed. But,—I heard him say that he thinks Wynne is in league with Mr. Stebbins and that the two of them brought about all the mysterious doings—"

"Hush, Milly! Don't let any one hear you! You mustn't breathe such things!"

"But he did say so, didn't he, Rudolph?"

"I won't tell you."

"I know he did! I heard him."

"Then forget it, as soon as you can. Trust me, Milly. I'll do all I can to keep suspicion from Wynne. But, do this, Milly. Use all your powers of persuasion with Professor Hardwick, and make him give up his plan of getting that detective up here. That Wise is a wise one indeed! He'll find out every thing we don't want known, and more, too! Will you, Milly, *will* you,—if only for Wynne's sake—try to keep that man away?"

"I'll try, Rudolph, oh, of course I will! But what can I do, if the Professor has made up his mind? You know how determined he is."

"Get the girls to help. Don't breathe to them a word that you overheard Peterson say, but manage to make them do all they can to keep that detective off. If you all band together, you can do it. Wynne won't want him; I don't; I don't think Mr. Tracy will; and if you women are on our side, Hardwick will be only one against the rest of us, and we must win the day! Milly, that Wise must *not* come up here,—if you value your peace of mind!"

"Oh, Rudolph, you frighten me so. I will do all I can, oh, I *will!*"

CHAPTER 13: PENNINGTON WISE

WHEN Mary Pennington married a man named Wise, it was not at all an unusual impulse that prompted her to name her first born son after her own family name, and so Pennington Wise came into being.

Then, of course, it followed, as the night the day, that his school chums should call him Penny Wise, which name stuck to him through life. Whether this significant name was the cause of his becoming a detective is not definitely known, but a detective he did grow up to be, and a good one, too. Eccentric, of course, what worthwhile detective is not? But clear cut of brain, mind and intelligence. And always on the lookout for an interesting case, for he would engage in no others.

Wherefore, his persistence in desiring to investigate the strange mysteries of Black Aspens won the day against Milly's endeavours to prevent his coming. She had done all she could, and most of the house party had aided her efforts, but Professor Hardwick had become imbued with the idea that there was human agency at work, and that his belief in spiritual visitation, honest though it had been, was doomed to a speedy death, unless further proof could be shown.

Norma, too, was rather inclined to welcome a specialist in the solving of mysterious problems, and in conference with the Professor agreed to do all she could to help the Wise man in his work. Norma was still of the opinion that the two tragic deaths were the work of evil spirits, but if it were not so, she wanted to know it.

But the principal reason why Pennington Wise came to Black Aspens was his own determination to do so. He had never heard of such an unusual and weird mystery, and it whetted his curiosity by its strange and almost unbelievable details.

The opposing party gave in gracefully, when they found his advent was inevitable. All but Milly, that is. She spent her time alternately crying her heart out in Wynne's arms, and bracing herself up for a calm and indifferent attitude before the new investigator.

"Keep a stiff upper lip," Braye advised her. "Remember not to give out any information, Milly. Let him find out all he can, but don't help him."

"All right, Rudolph; and, anyway, I know Wynne is innocent,—"

"Of course he is! That goes without saying. But if he is suspected, say, if Stebbins or Thorpe or anybody else puts Wise up to suspicion, it may mean a bad quarter of an hour for all of us. So, just be quiet, dignified, pleasant mannered and all that, but don't say anything definite. For it might be misconstrued and misunderstood, and make trouble. At least, that's the course I'm going to pursue, and I think it's the best plan."

"Oh, I know it is," Milly agreed. "In fact, that's just about what Wynne told me; he thinks if I try to help, I'll only make mistakes, so he, too, told me to keep quiet. Eve is awfully angry, because that man is coming. She's not saying so, but I know her! And, Rudolph, she's afraid of something. I don't know what, exactly, but she's fearfully afraid of developments."

"We all are, Milly. If the detective pins it on any human being,—that means trouble, and if he decides it's spooks, after all,—I think I'll be more afraid of them than ever!"

"I can't be any more afraid of them than I am!" Milly shuddered. "Oh, Rudolph, how I wish we had never come up here!"

"We all wish that, Milly, but as we're in for it now, we must see it through."

Pennington Wise arrived the next afternoon. He came into the hall like an army with banners. A tall, well set up man, of about thirty three or four, thick chestnut hair, worn a la brosse, clear blue eyes, a clean cut, fine featured face, and a manner that proclaimed generalship and efficiency to the last degree.

"Here I am," he announced, setting down several pieces of hand luggage and whipping off his soft gray felt hat. "You are the hostess?"

His quick darting eyes had picked out Milly, and he greeted her as a distinguished visitor might.

"Who is that?" exclaimed Milly, looking at a slight, black haired girl who followed quietly in Wise's footsteps.

"That? oh that's Zizi,—part of my luggage. Put her any place. Is there a housekeeper person? Yes? Well, turn Zizi over to her, she'll be all right."

Hester was peeping in at a rear door, unable to restrain her curiosity as to the commotion, and Zizi glided toward her and disappeared in the shadows.

"Now," said Wise, his quick smile flashing inclusively at all of them, "we must get acquainted. I'm Penny Wise, and all possible jokes on my name have already been made, so that's all right. I know Mrs. Landon, and you, of course," looking at Wynne, "are her husband. Professor Hardwick," and he bowed slightly, "is the man with whom I have had a short correspondence regarding my coming here. You, sir,—" he looked inquiringly at Braye.

"I'm Rudolph Braye, nephew of Mr. Gifford Bruce, and present heir to his fortune." The quiet sadness of Braye's tone precluded any idea of his triumph of exultation at the fact he stated. "This," he went on, "is the Reverend Mr. Tracy, a friend of us all. And these ladies are Miss Carnforth and Miss Cameron, both deeply interested in the solution of the mysteries that confront us. Since introductions are in order, may I inquire further concerning the young lady,—or child,—who accompanied you?"

"Zizi? She's part of my working outfit. In fact, one of my principal bits of paraphernalia. I always use her on mysterious cases. Don't look on her as an individual, please, she's a property,—in the theatrical sense, I mean."

"But her standing in the household?" asked Milly, "does she belong with the servants, or in here with us?"

"She'll look after that herself," and Penny Wise smiled. "Pay no more attention to her than you would to my umbrella or walking stick. Now we know each others' names, let's proceed to the case itself. Who is going to tell me all about it?"

"Which of us would you rather have do so?" asked Eve, her long, glittering eyes fixed on the detective's face.

He glanced at her quickly, and then let his gaze continue to rest on her beautiful, sibylline countenance.

"Not you," he said, "you are too—well, I suppose the word I must use is temperamental, but it's a word I hate."

"Why?" asked the Professor, "what do you mean by temperamental?"

"That's the trouble," smiled Wise. "It doesn't mean anything. Strictly speaking, every one has temperament of one sort or another, but it has come to mean an emotional temperament,—"

"What do you mean by emotional?" interrupted Hardwick.

"There you go again!" and Wise looked amused. "Emotions are of all sorts, but emotional has come to be used only in reference to demonstrations of the affections."

"You're a scholar!" cried the Professor. "Rarely do I meet a man with such a fine sense of terminology!"

"Glad you're pleased. But, Professor, neither do I choose you as historian of the affairs of Black Aspens. Let me see," his eyes roved from one to another, "it seems to me I'll get the most straightforward, uncoloured statement from a clerical mind. I think Mr. Tracy can tell me, in the way I want to hear it, a concise story of the mysteries and tragedies you have been through up here."

Mr. Tracy looked at the detective gravely.

"I am quite willing to do what I can," he said, "and I will tell the happenings as I know them. For occasions when I was not present, or where my memory fails, the others will, I trust, be allowed to help me out."

And then, the whole matter was laid before the intelligence of Pennington Wise, and with a rapt Jock of interest and a few pointed questions here and there, the detective listened to the history of his new case.

At last, the account having been brought up to date, Wise nodded his head, and sat silent for a moment. It was not the melodramatic silence of one affecting superiority, but the more impressive quietude of a mind really in deep thought.

Then Wise said, simply, "I've heard nothing yet to make me assume any supernatural agency. 'Ve you, Zizi?"

"No," came a soft, thin voice from the shadowy depths of the rear hall.

Milly jumped. "Has she been there all the time?" she said.

"She's always there," returned Wise, in a matter of fact way. "Now I'm ready to declare that the deaths of your two friends are positively not due to spiritistic wills, but are dastardly murders, cleverly accomplished by human hands and human brains."

"How?" gasped Eve Car n forth. She was leaning forward, her beryl eyes dilated and staring, her hands clenched, her slender form trembling with excitement.

"That I do not know yet,—do you, Zizi?"

"No," came tranquilly from the distance.

"Let that girl come here," cried Milly, pettishly. "It gets on my nerves to have her speaking from way back there!"

"Come here, Zizi," directed Penny Wise, and the slim young figure glided toward them. She was a mere slip of a girl, a wisp of humanity, in a flimsy frock of thin black stuff, with a touch of coral-tinted chiffon in bodice and sash. The skirt was short, and her black silk stockings and high heeled pumps gave her a chic air. Her black hair was drawn smoothly back, in the prevailing mode, and though she had an air of world knowledge, she was inconspicuous in effect.

Without a glance at the people, personally, she sat down in a chair, a little apart, yet in full view of all.

Wise paid no attention to her, and went on, thoughtfully. "No, there is no evidence pointing to the occult, but innumerable straws to show which way the camel's back is to be broken."

"Mr. Wise," said Eve, determinedly, "I don't think it is fair for you to hear the story only from, Mr. Tracy. I think he is opposed to a belief in psychics and so unintentionally colours his narrative to lead away from such theories."

"That may be so," said Tracy, himself, looking thoughtfully at Eve; "and I agree it would be fairer to hear the story, or parts of it, retold by Miss Carnforth or some one who fully believes in spiritism."

"Right," said Wise; "go ahead, Miss Carnforth, tell me anything that seems to you different in meaning from what Mr. Tracy has described."

Quite willing, Eve told of the ghostly visitant that had appeared to her the night she slept in the Room with the Tassels, and then described vividly the ghost that had appeared to Vernie, as Vernie had told it to her.

"You see," she concluded, "there is no explanation for these things, other than supernatural, for the locks and bars on the house preclude intrusion of outsiders, and all the occupants of the house are accounted for. I tell you the things just as they happened."

"With no wish to he discourteous, Miss Camforth, I would advise you to tell those tales to the submarines. Even the marines couldn't swallow those! Could they, Zizi?"

"No," and now that they could see the girl, all noticed a slight smile of amusement on her young face. It was quickly followed by a look of horror in her black eyes, as she murmured, "What awful frights you must have had!"

and she glanced at Milly, in sympathy. Then she turned toward Norma, and seemed about to speak, but thought better of it.

Not looking toward his "property," Wise went on talking. "I can readily see how any one willing to believe in the occult could turn these weird happenings into plausible proof. But it is not so. Miss Carnforth's own story convinces me even more strongly that there has been diabolical cleverness used, but by a human being, not a phantom."

"And you will discover how, you will solve the mysteries?" asked the Professor, eagerly.

"I hope to. But it is the most difficult appearing case I have ever encountered."

"It is not an eleventh case, then?" and Professor Hardwick told again of Andrew Lang's percentage of proof.

"No, it is not. It is one of the ten that are the result of fraud. Now to find the perpetrator of the fraud."

"At least you must admit, Mr. Wise," said Eve, a little spitefully, "that your saying it is a case of, fraud does not make it so."

"No," agreed Wise, smiling in an exasperatingly patronizing way, "it sure does not. In fact it has already made itself so."

"And your discovery of the means used is bound to come?" asked Tracy, with interest.

"Bound to come," repeated the detective. "But don't let us begin by being at odds with each other. I came here to discover the truth. If any one wants the truth to remain undiscovered, now is the time to say so. For it will soon be too late."

"Why should any one want the truth to remain undiscovered?" said Braye, abruptly.

"For two reasons," replied Wise, seriously. "First, any one criminally implicated might wish it to remain unknown; second, any one wishing to shield another, might also wish no discoveries made."

"But you don't think any of us are criminally implicated, I hope," and Braye looked questioning.

"There are others in this house beside you people," Wise returned; "and I tell you frankly, I'm not ready yet to suspect any one or even imagine who the criminal may be. I only state positively that disembodied spirits are not responsible for those two tragic deaths. Also, may I ask you to remember, that I've only just arrived, that I've had a tiresome journey, that I'd like rest and refreshment, and that there are more days coming for my further work."

"Why, bless my soul!" exclaimed the Professor, "that's all true! Do you know, Mr. Wise, it seems as if you'd always been here, it seems as if you were already one of us."

"Thank you, sir, that's a pleasant compliment to my personality, anyway. And now, if you please, Mrs. Landon, may I be shown to my room?"

"Certainly," said Milly, and she rang for Thorpe, as Landon rose to escort the guest himself.

"Where's that girl?" said Norma, looking round after the detective had gone off, "what became of her?"

But there was no sight of the little black robed figure.

"Oh, let her alone," said Eve, "she slid out to the kitchen, I think. Hester will look after her. That man said to pay no more attention to her than to his hand luggage. She'll look out for herself, I've no doubt. Isn't she awful, anyway?"

"I think she's pretty," said Norma, "in a weird, elfin sort of way."

"She knows it all," said Braye. "I never saw such an effect of old head on young shoulders in my life. But what a funny way to treat her."

"She's a spy," declared Eve, "that's what she is, a spy! With her silent, gliding ways, and her sly, soft voice! I hate her!"

"Now, now, Evie, don't be unjust!" and Braye smiled at her. "She is a bit your style and temperament, but don't be jealous!"

"Nonsense!" and Eve laughed back at him, "why, she isn't a bit like me! She has black hair and eyes—"

"I didn't notice," said Braye, "but she impressed me as being like you in lines and motions."

"A pocket edition," laughed Tracy. "Miss Carnforth would make two of that little shrimp, and Miss Carnforth is a sylph, herself."

The party broke up into smaller groups, and Braye and Norma sauntered off for their usual afternoon stroll.

Eve watched them go, her eyes moodily staring. "Won't I do?" said Tracy's quiet voice, and Eve pulled herself together and smiled at him.

"You're the one I want most," she declared gaily, unwilling to be thought disappointed. "Let's walk down by the lake."

The walk by the lake was always shaded, but as the day was murky it was gloomier than ever.

"You like this place?" asked Tracy, with a glance at the black grove of aspens, and their dark reflection in the still water of the deep pool.

"Yes, I do; or, I did, until that man came up here. There's no use in pursuing our investigations with him around."

"All the more use," declared Tracy. "If any supernatural things happen it will refute his cocksure decisions."

"Yes, it would. Oh, I do wish a ghost would appear to him, and scare him out of his wits!"

"He has plenty of wits, Miss Carnforth, and he'd take some scaring, I think. But if a real phantasm came, he'd know it, and he'd acknowledge it, I'm sure. He strikes me as an honourable man, and a decent, straightforward sort."

"If he is," and Eve ruminated, "perhaps he can help us to investigate—"

"That's what he's here for."

"I mean investigate *our* beliefs. If he could be convinced, as we are, of the existence of phantoms, and of their visitations, he'd be a splendid help, wouldn't he? Perhaps I am in wrong in disliking him."

"You're certainly premature. Why, not one man out of a thousand does believe in the occult. And not one in a million detectives, I daresay."

Meantime, Braye and Norma were talking in like vein.

"I do believe it was a spirit that killed our dear Vernie, and Mr. Bruce," Norma declared, "but if Mr. Wise can prove the contrary, we want him to do so, don't we, Rudolph?"

"Of course, Norma, we all feel that way. I, especially, for as heir to Uncle Gif's money, I'm in a peculiar position. But if anybody can get at the truth, this Wise person can. He's a live wire, I can see that."

"Shall we help him, Rudolph, or hold back and let him work alone?"

"Help him, of course! Why not? But, be careful that it is help we offer him, and not merely stupid interference."

"What do you mean by that?"

"Nothing particular; but some of us are inclined to be a bit officious, and—oh, I don't know, Norma,—I don't want to say anything—even to you. Let's talk of pleasanter subjects."

"What, for instance?"

"You, for instance! You're enchanting to day, in that pale blue gown. It makes you look like an angel."

"Do they wear pale blue?"

"I don't know what they wear, and shan't care until you really are one, and then, I hope I'll be one, too. But you look like an angel, because of your angelic face. It's like a roseleaf washed in sunlight—"

"Now, Rudolph, don't try to be poetical! You can't hit it off! A washed face is remindful of a soap advertisement,—not an angel!"

"Rogue! You love to make fun of me! But I don't mind. Oh, Norma, I don't care what you say to me, if you'll only say yes. Won't you, dearest?"

"Bad boy! Behave yourself! I told you not to ask *any* question until we get away from this place. I won't listen to love talk at Black Aspens! It's out of the picture!"

"But will you, as soon as we get back to New York? Will you, Norma—darling?"

"Wait till then, and we'll see," was all the answer he could get.

CHAPTER 14: ZIZI

"WHERE is she?" Milly asked of Hester, as, more out of curiosity than hospitality she went to the kitchen.

"Well! Mis' Landon, I never see such a thing in all my born days! She slid out here like she was on roller skates! 'Hester?' she says, smilin', and with that she settled herself for good and all, 'sif she'd been born an' brought up here! She slid to the cupboard, and picked out the tea caddy, and took down a little teapot, and in a jiffy, she'd snatched up the b'ilin' teakettle, and was settin' at that there table, drinkin' her tea! I got her out some cakes, and by then she was a cuttin' bread an' butter! Never 've I seen her like!"

"Did she trouble you?"

"Land, no, ma'am! She waits on herself, but so quick, you'd think she was a witch!"

"Where is she now?"

"Well, ma'am, she finished her tea, and then she fair scooted up the back stairs. I heard her dart into one or two rooms, and then she took the little South gable room for hers. I could hear her stepping about, putting her things away, I make no doubt. She looked in here again, a minute, and said, 'I've chosen that little room with the lattice wall paper,' and then she disappeared again. That's all I know about her. No, ma'am, she don't trouble me none, and I don't say I don't sort o' take to her. But she's a queer little piece. She is that."

Milly sighed. "Every thing's queer, Hester," she said, broodingly, and then she went back to the hall.

Wynne Landon sat there alone. His face was grave, and he sighed deeply as his wife came to him and laid her hand on his shoulder.

"Where's everybody, Wynnsie?" she said cheerily.

"Traipsing over the house, hunting clues! Rotten business, Milly."

"Why? What do you mean by that?"

"Nothing. I hope if that man is going to find the criminal, he'll make short work of it!"

"So do I, dear, then we can go home, can't we?"

"You bet! Here they are, now,—they seem in good spirits."

The crowd came down the stairs and into the great hall, laughing at some quip of Wise's. Ever since the day of the two deaths a sombre gloom had pervaded the whole place, and smiles had been few. The sound of laughter came as a shock to the Landons, but the cheery face of Penny Wise betokened only wholesome good nature, and not flippant heartlessness.

"Old Montgomery knew how to build a house," he commented, looking at the finely curving staircase, and its elaborate balusters. "Living rooms nowadays are all very well, but these great entrance halls are finer places to congregate. You spend much of your time here, I'm sure. The worst part is, they're difficult to light properly,—by daylight, I mean. And, you've no electrics here, have you?"

"No," replied Landon, "only kerosene and candles. You see, the place has been unoccupied for years."

"Haunted houses are apt to be,—"

"Reputed haunted houses," corrected the Professor.

"There are no others," and Wise grinned. "All reputed haunted houses have nothing to haunt them but their repute. I mean, the story of their ghost is all the ghost they have."

"But I saw the ghost here," and Eve spoke with a quiet dignity that defied contradiction.

"Of course you did," Wise assented. "The ghost came purposely to be seen."

"Did you ever see one, Mr. Wise?"

"I never did, Miss Carnforth, I never hope to see one! But I can tell you anyhow, I'd rather see than be one."

"Oh, of course, if you're going to take that tone," and Eve turned away, decidedly offended.

"Sorry!" and Wise flashed a smile at her. "But, you see, a detective can't afford to believe in ghosts. We make our living solving mysteries, and to say, 'It was the ghost! You're right, it was the ghost!' is by way of begging the question."

"Then you think the phantoms that appeared to some of us were really human beings?" asked Tracy, interestedly.

"I sure do."

"And you propose to find out who and how?" said Braye.

"If I live up to my reputation, I must do so. There are but two kinds of detectives. Effective detectives and defective detectives. It is the aim of my life to belong to the former class, and here's my chance to make good. Now, I've examined the Upper floors, I'll look over this hall and the ground floor rooms. Shall I have time before dinner, Mrs. Landon?"

His charm and pleasant personality had already won Milly's liking and she said, cordially, "Yes, indeed, Mr. Wise. And if you wish, we'll delay dinner to suit your pleasure."

"Not at all. Done in a few minutes. Stunning hall, eh, Zizi?"

"Yes," said the thin little voice of the thin little girl, and Milly suddenly realized that Zizi was present with the crowd.

The graceful little figure stepped forward and stood at Wise's side as he looked the hall over. He tapped at the panelled walls, and smiled as he said, "Solid and intact. No secret passage or sliding panel,—of that I'm sure."

"If you're trying to find a secret entrance into the house, Mr. Wise," Landon said, "you are wasting your time. I am more or less architecturally inclined, and I've tapped and sounded and measured and calculated,—and I can assure you there's nothing of the sort."

"Good work! That saves me some trouble, I'm sure. Marvellous work on these doors, eh? And the bronze columns,—from abroad, I take it."

"Yes;" Professor Hardwick said, slapping his hand against one of the fluted bronze pillars, "I admire these columns more than the doors even. They're unique, I don't wonder their owner 'built a house behind them.' I doubt if their match is in America."

"And the locks and bolts are as ponderous as the doors," commented the detective. "Eh, Zizi?"

"They are like that all over the house," said the girl, in a casual tone. "Even the kitchen quarters are as securely fastened and bolted. And upstairs, any doors that give on balconies are strongly guarded. I have never seen a house more carefully looked after in the matter of barricades."

The girl spoke slowly, as if on the witness stand. Then suddenly her black eyes twinkled, and she turned sharply toward Eve, saying, "Oh, do you do that, too?"

"Do what?" cried Eve, angrily. "What do you mean?"

"Scribble notes, and pass 'em to somebody. I do, too. It's a habit I can't seem to break myself of."

"I didn't!" and Eve's face flushed and her eyes glittered with a smouldering fire.

"Oh, tra la la," trilled Zizi, and nonchalantly turned away.

"Now for the Room with the Tassels," said Wise, and led the way to the fateful room.

"Ghastly, ghostly and grisly!" he declared after a quick survey, "but no entrance except by door or windows."

"And they were locked every time the room was slept in by any of our party," announced the Professor, positively.

"That makes it easier," smiled Wise. "You see, I feared secret panels and that sort of thing,—not uncommon in old houses. But you've found none?"

"None," asseverated Landon. "If your theory of a human 'ghost' is right, you've got to account for the forcing of the big bolts of those front door—"

"Or suspect some of your household," conclude Wise, practically. "Well, I haven't suspected any one as yet; I'm just absorbing facts, on which to base my theories. Now, for the drawing room."

The long sombre, old fashioned room received scant examination.

"Nothing doing, Zizi?" said Wise, briefly.

"Only a Bad Taste Exhibition," the girl remarked, making a wry face at the ornate decorations and appointments. Then, with her peculiar, gliding motion, she slid across the hall again, and examined the knob and lock on the door of the Room with the Tassels.

"Fascinating room," she said, with a glance round it. "But horrible," and her thin shoulders shrugged. "Those tassels are enough to make a hen cross the road!"

Milly giggled, and for the first time since the day of the tragedies.

Dinner was rather pleasant than otherwise. The detective, laying aside all thought or talk of his purpose there, was entertaining and even merry. He spoke somewhat of himself, and it transpired that he was an artist,—an illustrator of current magazine stories.

"And Zizi is my model," he informed them, "that is, when I want a thin, scarecrow type. I don't use her for the average peach heroine. Look Ziz, don't eat too much of that potato puff! see, if she puts on a bit of flesh, she runs straight back to the movie studios."

"Ah, a film star?" said Braye.

"Not a star," and Wise shook his head. "But a good little actress for a brat part."

Zizi flashed an amused smile from her black eyes and partook again of the forbidden potato puff.

"Zizi! For the love of Mike!" expostulated Wise.

"The love of Mike is the root of all evil," said Zizi, saucily; "but then, everything is."

"Is what?" asked Eve, interested against her will in this strange child.

"Is the root of all evil," was the calm reply.

"Whew! this must be an evil old world!" exclaimed Braye.

"And isn't it?" Zizi flashed back, her big eyes sparkling like liquid jet.

"Are you a pessimist, little one?" asked the Professor, studying the clever, eerie face.

"Nay, nay, Pauline," and the small, pointed chin was raised a bit. "Not so, but far otherwise."

"Then why do you think the world is evil?"

"Ah, sir, when one spends one's life between a Moving Picture Studio and a popular artist's studio, one learns much that one had better left unlearnt."

The child face suddenly looked ages old, and then, as suddenly broke into a gay smile: "Don't ask me these things," she said, "ask Penny Wise. I'm only his Pound Foolish."

"You'll put on another foolish pound if you eat any more of that dessert," growled Wise, scowling at her.

"All right, I won't," and the slender little fingers laid down the teaspoon Zizi was using. Then, in an audible aside, she added, "Hester will give me more, later," and chuckled like a naughty child.

The next morning Pennington Wise set about his work in earnest. "I'm going to East Dryden," he announced. "I want to interview the doctors, also Mr. Stebbins. I don't mind saying frankly, this is the deepest mystery I have ever encountered. If any of you here can help me, I beg you will do so, for the case looks well nigh hopeless. Ah, there, Zizi."

The girl appeared, ready to go with Wise in the motor car. She wore a small black hat with an oriole's wing in it, and a full draped black cape, whose flutterings disclosed an orange coloured lining. Inconspicuous, save when the cape's lining showed, Zizi looked distinguished and smartly costumed. A small black veil, delicately adjusted, clouded her sharp little features, and she sprang into the car without help, and nestled into a corner of the tonneau.

Only a chauffeur accompanied them, and he could not hear the conversation carried on in low tones.

"What about it, Ziz?" murmured Wise, as they passed the aspen grove and the black lake.

"Awful doings," she returned, merely breathing the words. "The Eve girl has a secret, too."

"Too?"

"Yes, she isn't the criminal, you know."

"I don't know."

"Well, you will know. She's a queer mechanism, but she never killed anybody."

"Sure, Zizi?"

"Sure, oh, Wise Guy. Now, who did do it?"

"Well, who did?"

"We don't know yet, and we mustn't theorize without data, you know."

"Rats! I always theorize without data. And I've never failed to corral the data."

"You're a deuce of a deducer, you are!"

"And you're a She Sherlock, I suppose! Well, oh, Mine of Wisdom, go ahead. Spill it to me."

"Can't now. I've lost my place! But, after a few more interviews with some few more interested parties, I may, perhaps, possibly, maybe,—oh, Penny, look back at the house from here! Did you ever see such a weird, wild spook pit!"

Black Aspens did indeed look repellent. No one was in sight, and the grove of black, waving trees, mirrored in the deep black shadows of the lake gave it all a doomed effect that the dull, leaden sky intensified.

The grim old house seemed the right anode for evil spirits or uneasy wraiths, and Zizi, fascinated by the still scene continued to gaze backward until a turn of the road hid it from view.

Then she became silent, and would vouchsafe no answer to Wise's questions or make any remarks of her own.

During the interview between the detective and Elijah Stebbins, she said almost nothing, her big eyes staring at the owner of Black Aspens, until the old man writhed in discomfort.

"How did you get in?" she shot at him, as he frankly admitted his harmless tricks to give his tenants their desired interest in his house.

"I was in, miss," Stebbins said, nervously twisting his fingers; "I staid there the first night, and 'twas then I moved the old candlestick."

"I don't mean that," and Zizi's eyes seemed to bore through to his very brain, "I mean the night you played ghost."

"Why,—I—that is,—they left a window open—"

"They did not!" Zizi shot at him, "and you know it! How did you get in?"

But old Stebbins persisted in his story of entrance by an overlooked window.

"There's heaps of windows in that house," he declared. "Land, I could get in any time I wanted to."

"Sure you could," retorted Zizi, "but not through a window!"

"How, then?" said Stebbins.

"That's what I asked you. I know."

"You know! *How* do you know?"

"Your mama told my mama and my mama told me!" Zizi's mocking laughter so incensed the old man that he shook with fury.

"You don't know!" he cried, "'cause there's nothin' to know! Land! All them folks up there has hunted the place for secret entrances, and I ruther think you have too," and he nodded at Wise.

"I have," said Wise, frankly, "and I've discovered none as yet. But, listen here, friend Stebbins, if there is one, I will find it,—and that's all there is about that!—"

Zizi said nothing, having returned to her taciturn role, but the glance she threw at Stebbins, he said afterward, made his blood run cold.

"She's a witch cat!" he declared to his cronies, when telling the tale, "she ain't all human,—or I'm a sinner!"

On their way to see Dan Peterson, Wise inquired concerning Zizi's knowledge of a secret way to get into the house.

"A small bluff," she said, carelessly. "I dunno how he got in, I'm sure. But I don't believe those people left a window conveniently open, unless—they did it on purpose. Who does the locking up, do you know?"

"Mr. Landon, I believe."

"Quite so! It's a pity, isn't it Pen, how everything appears to wind around back to that nice Mr. Landon!"

"Well, what now?"

"Well, if he and Stebbins were in cahoots—"

"Hold up, Zizi, don't run away with yourself! You're a day ahead of the fair. Now, are you going to talk, in here at Peterson's, or sit like a bump on a log,—smiling at grief?"

"I dunno; which would you?"

"Talk," said Wise, succinctly, and Zizi talked. Indeed, she carried on the main part of the conversation, which was exactly what Wise had meant tor her to do.

She charmed Peterson with her bright, alert air and her pleasant, quick witted way of putting things.

Together they went over the known details, and then she cleverly drew from Peterson his deductions and decisions.

At first, inclined to resent the advent of this all-wise detective, he now began to think that if they could work together, he would shine by reflected glory, that is, if the new chap succeeded in solving the mystery, which to him was inexplicable.

"I can't suspect the Thorpes or Mr. Stebbins," Peterson finally declared: "I did think I could, but though Eli did cut up some tricks, they were harmless and merely in fun. And, too, he has absolute alibis for all the spook appearances after a certain date. And that's the date when that Miss Carnforth saw a ghost. As near as I can make out, that ghost was Stebbins himself, but no spooks after that was Stebbins' doings. Now, I give you that straight and simple, Mr. Wise, but it took me a long time to ferret it out. I suspected it, but I've had hard work to get Stebbins to admit his tricks, and also to check up his alibis after that particular night."

"These perfectly attested alibis are sometimes manufactured very carefully," said Zizi, fixing her black eyes on Peterson.

"Yes, they are. That's why I checked up Eli's so carefully. But they're all true. I've got an exact list of the spook performances from the people at the house. I got the data from different ones, at different times, so's to be sure they were all there. Then, I looked up Stebbins' whereabouts on each occasion, and as I tell you, after the night he owns up to playing ghost, he never did it again."

"Then did he arrange for the Thorpes or one of the waiting maids to do it?" queried Zizi.

"That I can't say. I think he must have done so, but I can't find a scrap of proof, nor is there any motive. Stebbins is a good old sort and he honestly wanted to give his tenants the ha'nts, as he calls 'em, that they wanted. But why, on this good green earth, he should want to kill two of them is unanswerable. No, take it from me, Eli Stebbins is no murderer. I've looked up his record and his life story, and there's no indication that he knew any of these people before they came up here, so he couldn't have had any old grudge or family feud or anything of that sort. Stebbins isn't the criminal, no sir ee!"

"I never thought he was," said Wise, quietly. "You've done good work Mr. Peterson, and you've saved me a heap of trouble in getting these facts so undeniably established. I thank you, and I shall be glad of your cooperation in my further work."

"Good for you, I'll be right down glad to work with you. And this young lady, Mr. Wise, is she one of us?"

"She *is* us," returned Wise, simply. "Don't bother about her, Mr. Peterson, she's the sort that looks after herself. Report to me, please, if you discover anything new."

CHAPTER 15: TRACY'S STORY

I wouldn't say," Wise observed, "that there is no such thing as occult phenomena—"

"What do you mean by phenomena?" interrupted the Professor. "Not one person in ten uses that word correctly."

"I'm that single and unique one, old top," Wise assured him, "for my exact meaning, see Webster; but I was going to say, even granting the possibility of the two deaths being due to supernatural causes, I'm not going to accept that solution of the mystery until I've exhausted all other available means of finding a flesh and blood murderer, which same I strongly expect to find."

"He'll do it," said Zizi, addressing the others, while her black eyes looked at Wise as at an inanimate object. "He's an effective detective, firsy last and all the time. And I'm the little cog that makes the wheels go round. So, I think, Teckyteck, that I'll carry out a plan I've just thought of. I'll move from the pretty little bedroom I now occupy, and sleep in the Room with the Tassels."

"Oh, don't!" cried Norma. "Something might happen to you!"

"That's what I'm flattering myself. And it's nice of you, Miss Cameron, to speak out like that." Zizi's eyes flashed a quizzical glance at Eve, who was nodding satisfaction at the proposed plan.

Eve coloured and dropped her eyes, and Zizi went on. "You see, people, Mr. Wise can't size up these ghosts of yours unless he sees them,—and for me to see them is the same thing. So I'm going to take the haunted room for my own and if the Shawled Woman appears, I'll pin a tag on her shawl."

Norma shuddered. "Don't talk like that," she begged. "You don't know what risk you run. Milly, don't let the child sleep there."

But all objections were overruled, and Zizi quietly transferred her few simple belongings to the Room with the Tassels.

At breakfast, the morning after her first night in the haunted room, she declared she had never slept better or more soundly, that there had been no disturbance of any kind, and that she adored the room.

"You saw and heard nothing?" queried Eve, looking at her intently.

"Nixy," and the pert little face was all smiles.

"But the game isn't out till it's played out, you know."

"I fail to grasp the cryptic meaning of that remark," said Eve, with an insolent stare at Zizi.

"Same here!" and the child's eerie laugh rang out. "But when I don't know exactly what to say, I sing out some old saw like that."

Zizi's laugh was infectious, and Milly giggled in sympathy, while the others smiled too.

"The experience was mine, last night," said Mr. Tracy, in his deep, resonant voice. "I suppose I'd better tell of it."

"By all means," said Penny Wise, as the clergyman hesitated.

"A phantom appeared to me," Tracy began, "just as the hall clock struck four. I wasn't asleep, of that I'm sure, but I was suddenly aware of a presence in the room. A tall, misty shape seemed to take form as I looked, and it had the appearance of a woman with a shawl over her head. She drew near to me, and I could see her face, and it was that of a skull. I was stunned, rather than frightened, and when I tried to call out, I could make no sound. The thing faded away as gradually as it had appeared, and after a time I regained a normal state of nerves. I don't want to be an alarmist, or frighten anybody, but I—well, I confess I didn't enjoy the experience, and I take occasion to say now, that I shall leave here to day. I'm going to Boston, and will return at any time, if for any reason my presence is desired or my affidavit wanted as a witness. You all know what I've thought about this whole matter. While not a spiritualist, I've preserved an open mind toward any revelations we may have had, and I'm always ready to be convinced. And I may say the sight I saw last night has gone far to convince me. But I don't care to see it again," Tracy shuddered, "and at risk of being thought cowardly, I've determined to go away. I had intended to go shortly, anyway, and I prefer to go to day."

"I don't blame you, old chap," said Braye, heartily; "there's no reason why you should jeopardize your nervous system by exposing it to further shocks. Let Mr. Wise take down the details of your story, keep in touch with us as to your whereabouts and where we can communicate with you, and go ahead. I don't blame you one bit. In fact, if any one else wants to leave, no objections will be made. How about you, Professor?"

"I want to stay, please. I'm terribly interested in the matter, and I think Mr. Wise is making progress, and will make more, rapidly. I'm anxious to stay."

"I'm game, too," said Landon. "In fact I think we all want to see it through, except Mr. Tracy, and he is not so closely associated with the case as the rest of us."

So Tracy went, about noon of that day, and left an address that he said would always reach him, wherever he might be temporarily.

Milly and Norma regretted his going, for they had come to like the grave, kindly man, but Eve seemed not to care; and the men were all so interested in the work of Penny Wise, that they only gave a hearty good bye and Godspeed to the departing cleric.

"Queer, that spook should appear to him," said Wise, after Mr. Tracy had gone.

"He told me some time ago," said Norma, reminiscently, "that he often heard strange sounds at four in the morning. He said they were like faint moans and rustlings and sometimes a soft step along the halls."

"Did he ever see anything before?" asked Zizi.

"I don't think so. He was not very communicative about it, anyway. I think he was nervous on the subject."

"I know he was," Eve spoke scornfully. "He was afraid, I'm positive. No one ought to have joined this party who was afraid."

"We only asked him to fill in, you know," said Milly, rather apologizing for the minister's timidity. "And goodness knows, *I'm* afraid! Or I should be, if Wynne weren't always with me. If that thing appeared to me,— well!"

Milly could find no words to express her horror, and Landon looked at her anxiously.

"It won't," said Zizi, reassuringly, "it won't, Mrs. Landon."

"How do you know?" said Eve, a bit abruptly.

"Your mama told my mama and my mama told me," returned Zizi, who could put such graphic impudence into the silly phrase, that it was impossible not to be amused at it. "Oh, do you do that, too?" she added, as Eve bit her lip in annoyance. "So do I! It's such a hard habit to break, ain't it? But you oughtn't to, it scars your lips. Now, Penny Wise, if you'll go for a walk and a talk with your little otherwise, she'll tell you sumpum that you ought to know."

"Look out, Ziz," Wise said to her, as they walked off by themselves, and followed the path by the lake, "you mustn't be too saucy to Miss Carnforth, or there'll be trouble."

"Have to, honey. I've got to get her real mad at me, to find out her secret. She's no criminal, as I've told you, but she knows who is."

"Do you?"

"Not yet, but soon. Now, listen, while I expound a few. Friend Spook did appear to me last night."

"Really?"

"Sure as shootin'! I thought it over, and decided I'd better not admit it to the gaping crowd, or we'll never find out who does the stunt."

"But, really, Zizi?"

"Yes, really, Pen. It was about two o'clock,—not four. A tall shape, draped in white, breezed in and toddled around trying to attract my attention. I lay there and looked sort of glassy eyed, as if I was awake, but kinda hypnotized, you know. Well, I kept up that attitude, and the thing came nearer and leaned over me, and sure enough it had a skull for a face; but, land, Penny, it was a *papier mache* skull,—a mask, you know. 'T would be fine in the movies, I must put Manager Reeves up to that dodge!"

"Go on, Ziz."

"Well, the thing,—the person, I mean, for it was a real, live person all right,—sashayed around a bit, then gave a hollow groan,—I guess that's what they call hollow,—and slid out. That's all."

"You're a corker, Zizi! Why didn't you yell?"

"I wanted to see the game. Then, when the pleasant faced visitor left, I knew it was because I was supposed to have been sufficiently impressed. I thought it over, and I decided that at breakfast, I'd say I hadn't seen anything, and see who looked self conscious. And, by jiminy! nobody did! If any one around that table was my visiting spook, he or she carried it off something marvellous! Not one of 'em flickered an eyelash when I said I'd had a sweet, sound sleep all night. I can't see how any one could be so self controlled. Now, Penny, could it have been anybody who wasn't at the breakfast table?"

"Meaning Stebbins or the Thorpes?"

"Oh, no! none of them! But how about some outsider, hired, you know, by somebody in the house."

"How'd he get in?"

"There's a secret way into this house. You needn't tell me there isn't. Just 'cause you haven't stumbled over it yet! Also, who's doing the hiring?"

"You said everything came around toward Landon."

"There's motive there. You see, after Mr. Braye, Mr. Landon inherits all the Bruce fortune, and that's millions."

"What's the matter with Braye being the murderer? He inherits first."

"That's just it. If Mr. Braye wanted to kill his relatives to get the fortune, he wouldn't do it up here, where he's so liable to be suspected. He'd invent some subtler way, or some less suspicious scheme. But Mr. Landon could do it up here, and feel sure the suspicion would fall on Mr. Braye. Then, you see, Mr. Braye gets the money, and later on, Mr. Landon puts him out, too. In some awfully clever way, that can't be traced to him, d'y' see? And, too, Mr. Braye has declared he'll give all the money, if necessary, to discovering the criminal, if there is one. And he said, he'd give what was left to build a hospital. No, he doesn't want the money that came to him in such an awful way, leastwise, not if it throws suspicion on him. He's going to be cleared, or he's not going to use the money for himself. Miss Carnforth told me all that, I've talked a lot with her."

"You've talked with all of them, haven't you?"

"Yes, indeed. I've babbled on, and most often they tell me a lot that they don't realize. Mrs. Landon, now, she's struggling hard not to suspect her own husband, but Miss Carnforth has said a few things that scare Mrs. Landon 'most to death. Oh, Penny, it's a fearful case! We must fix it up, we must!"

"We will, Zizi. There's so much evidence not to be denied, that we must ferret out what it really means. I'm getting a glimmer, but your help is invaluable. That was a stroke of genius for you not to tell of your ghost! Weren't you frightened?"

"Not a bit. All I wanted to do, was to find out who it was. But I didn't dare grab at it, for I knew it would get away. I hope it will come again. I'll try to make it speak, and maybe I'll get a line on the voice."

"Was it a man or a woman?"

"I couldn't tell. The draperies were long and full, and the skull mask covered the face."

"Didn't you see the hand?"

"It was lost in the draped shawl. But I'm sure I'll have another visit, and then I'll get more information. You think I did well, oh, Wise Guy?"

"I do indeed!" and the approving smile that was Zizi's most welcome reward lighted up the detective's face.

Zizi pursued her plan of talking to the various people separately. She gleaned much this way and with her powers of lightning calculation, she put two and two together with astounding results.

She even lured the old Professor into a tete a tete conversation.

"No, I don't believe those deaths were supernatural, *now,*" he said, thoughtfully; "I did, but it's too incredible. However, it's no more unbelievable than that they could have been accomplished by human power."

"They were," and Zizi's black head nodded affirmation.

"How, then?"

"By a diabolically clever genius. Tell me again, Professor, just how those people were sitting? Were they together?"

"Mr. Bruce and Vernie? No. There was the width of the room between them."

"Were you near either?"

"Yes, sitting next to Mr. Bruce. We were talking absorbedly."

"Had he tasted his tea?"

"I think he had taken one sip,—not more, I'm sure."

"There was poison in that tea, Professor."

"There must have been, but how *could* there be?"

"Who gave it to him?"

"Let me see; Miss Carnforth presided, as Mrs. Landon was not at home. Miss Carnforth made the tea, and poured the cups, and Vernie and Mr. Tracy,—yes, and

Mr. Landon were passing the things around. It was all most informal, we never have the servants in at tea time. I couldn't really say just who did give Mr. Bruce his cup. Vernie gave me mine, I think."

"Well, the poison was put in Mr. Bruce's cup, after Miss Carnforth fixed it for him."

"Bless my soul, do you think so? That lets Braye out, then, for he wasn't there."

"You don't suspect Mr. Braye, do you?"

"No; of course not; but I don't really suspect anybody. But Mr. Braye is the heir, you know, and so may be said to have motive."

"That is true of Mr. Landon,—in a way."

"I can't suspect either of those two,—it's impossible."

"Go on, Professor, tell me about the little girl's death."

"You've heard it before."

"I know, but every little helps."

"She was across the room. I was looking at Bruce, of course, when I heard an exclamation —"

"From whom?"

"I don't know; Miss Carnforth, I think. Any way, she and Tracy were bending over Vernie,—they had laid her on a couch,—and in a moment, they said she was dead. At the same time, Mr. Bruce breathed his last. It was all so fearful, so terrible, we were stunned. At least, I was, and one by one we pulled ourselves together, trying to realize what had happened."

"All right, I know the rest. You've helped me a little— "

"Do you suspect anybody? Does Mr. Wise? Tell me, child. I can doubtless be of help, if I know what to do."

"No, Professor, you can't help. It's very awful, but it will soon be clear to all. Heaven help that poor Miss Carnforth."

"Nonsense! Eve didn't do it! Of that I'm certain."

"So am I. Of course, Miss Carnforth didn't do it. The tea was all right when she fixed Mr. Bruce's cup."

"Then who tampered with it? Not Vernie!"

But Zizi had run away. She had a way of making sudden exits and entrances, and one never knew where she was or when she would appear.

That night Zizi declared that she hoped the ghost would visit her. She said this openly, as the whole crowd were preparing to go to their rooms for the night.

"Perhaps it will," said Wise, looking at her, thoughtfully. "If it called on Mr. Tracy last night, it may be here again to night, and you may be favoured. Are you not afraid?"

"Not of the ghost," said Zizi, "but I am afraid that some of you people may play a trick just to scare me. Will you double up, so I can feel sure there's nothing of that sort?"

"I'll take Mr. Tracy's room," said Mr. Wise, "then I can keep my eye on Mr. Braye and Professor Hardwick. Though I've no mental image of either of them trailing round in sheets!"

"I should say not!" and Braye shuddered. "No, Miss Zizi, you've nothing to fear from us."

"Nor us," Norma assured her. "I was going to sleep in the room with Miss Carnforth, anyway, and that will preclude either of us impersonating a phantom."

"What an awful idea," and Eve glowered at Zizi. "You don't really think any of us would stoop to such a despicable thing, do you?"

"You never can tell," said Zizi, nonchalantly. "Mrs. Landon, you won't let your husband leave your room, will you?"

"No," said Milly, not at all resenting the question which Zizi put to her in a gentle, pleading tone, very different from that she had used to the others.

And so, the inmates of the house being accounted for, and the doors and windows looked after with extra care and precaution, the household settled itself to quietness, and the dark hours passed, ticked off and struck by the great deep toned clock in the hall.

It was between two and three, when Zizi, watching, perceived her door slowly and silently swing open.

Determined to learn all possible as to who the intruder could be, the girl lay motionless, but breathing deeply as if asleep.

Her eyes, almost closed, yet took in every movement of her silent visitor.

It was no white robed ghost, but a tall figure, clad in a long black cloak, and wearing a black mask. With a swift stride, that betokened a man, the figure approached the bed, having first softly closed the door that led to the hall.

Watching covertly for the next development, Zizi was all unprepared for what really happened.

The man, with a sudden, swift gesture, took the girl's chin in one strong hand, and opened her mouth, while with the other he thrust in a thick soft cloth, saturated with chloroform.

Not enough to make her lose her senses entirely, it partially stupefied her, and the choking cloth prevented all speech.

Whipping off the long dark cloak he wore, the man flung it round Zizi, as he lifted the slender form from the bed.

Vainly trying to emit a shriek, or utter a groan, Zizi fell, half conscious, back in the arms that supported her.

After an unknown interval, a draught of cool air on her face brought her back to a dim consciousness, and she realized she was out of doors. A struggle of her arms and legs resulted in a firmer grasp of the strong arms that carried her, and she quit moving, to think. She had been kidnapped, taken from her bed, and had been carried out of doors, but she had no knowledge of who her captor was nor by what means they had left the house. Her brain was furiously wide awake, but she made no move, lest more chloroform be administered, and she lose her regained consciousness.

On the shore of the black lake the man stopped, and set her on her feet. Her mouth, still filled with the soft cloth, was strained and painful, but the first attempt to raise her hand resulted in its being clutched by the strong hand of the man who swayed her destiny.

So slender and light was she, that he handled her as one might a child, and in his strong grasp she was as powerless as an infant.

Working quickly and deftly, he tied a strong rope round her ankles and to it attached what was only too evidently a bag of stones or bricks.

Then, without a word, he flung her into the deep, dark waters of the lake, and with one backward glance, he walked away.

CHAPTER 16: WHAT HAPPENED TO ZIZI

"JUST like a kitten!" Zizi sputtered; "just like a little, day old kitten! Ugh! I'm as mad as a wet hen!"

She was sitting on the bank of the lake, dripping wet, daubed with mud, her black eyes snapping with anger.

When she had been thrown into the pool, the big, entangling cape had caught in the sedge grass that bordered the water, and clutching this, the girl had hung on till she could manage to slip her slim little feet from the rope that bound them. A stiff rope and clumsily tied, it had been possible to free her self, though she might not have been able to do it, but for her experiences as a moving picture actress. It was not the first time she had been flung into water, for her slim agility had proved useful in film thrillers, and acrobatic feats were her long suit.

Able, too, to remain under water for a few moments without breathing, she had freed herself from the rope, and scrambled up the bank almost as rapidly as she had been sent to her intended doom.

She had pulled the cloth from her mouth, and sat, breathing in good air, but too exhausted to rise.

"If he'd only spoken, drat him!" she muttered, "and yet it must have been that wretch! I know it was, but how can I prove it? Oh, I wish it wasn't so dark! And I'm so *wet!*"

She got up now, and tried to wring the water from the cloak that she still clutched round her. Beside that she had on her nightdress, and a thin silk kimono, both of which were wetly clinging to her slim little body.

Throwing the still soaking wet cloak about her, and shivering as it sopped against her, she went toward the house.

It stood, still and sombre, a black thing amid blacker shadows. The aspen branches soughed eerily, but no other sound broke the silence. The great doors were closed, the windows all shut, and no sign of life was visible.

Zizi hesitated. Should she whistle beneath Penny Wise's window, or—

The alternative she thought of seemed to her best, and she drew her wet draperies about her and scuttled off at a smart pace toward the village.

Barefooted as she was, she chose grassy ground whenever possible, but her feet were sadly cut and bruised before she reached her destination.

This was the house of Dan Peterson, and a ring at his doorbell, brought the sound of a hastily flung up window, and a sharp "Who's there?"

"Me," said Zizi, truthfully, "please let me in."

Not quite certain of the identity of his caller, but touched by the pleading little voice, Peterson came downstairs, followed by his wife.

A few words of explanation resulted in Zizi's being put into warm, dry clothes, and tucked into bed by Mrs. Peterson, who admonished her to 'sleep like a baby till mornin'.'

Which, nothing loth, Zizi did.

Morning at Black Aspens brought a shock of surprise.

It was Hester who first discovered the absence of Zizi from the Room with the Tassels.

Hester had been fond of the child from the beginning, and in spite of her fifteen years, and her even older world knowledge, Zizi was a child, in many ways. Hester mothered her whenever possible, though Zizi's natural efficiency made little assistance really necessary. But Hester loved to wait on her, and so, this morning, when, going into the room with a can of hot water, she found no sleepy little occupant of the great bed, she ran straight upstairs to Miss Carnforth's room.

"Where's that child?" she demanded as Eve opened the door to her loud knock.

"What child? Who?"

"Zizi. She's gone! Sperrited away! What have you done with her?"

"Hush, Hester! You act crazy—"

"And crazy I am, if any harm's come to that girl! Where is she?"

Doors opened and heads were thrust out, as the voice of the irate Hester was heard about the house.

Penny Wise, in bathrobe and slippers, appeared, saying, "What's up? Zizi disappeared?"

"Yes," moaned Hester, "her bed's been slept in, but she ain't nowhere to be found. Oh, where can she be?"

"Be quiet," commanded Wise. He ran downstairs, and examined the doors and windows minutely. Except for those that Hester or Thorpe had opened that morning, all were locked as they had been left the night before.

"She may be in the house somewhere," suggested Norma, wide eyed and tearful.

"Not she," said Wise. "She would hear our commotion, and come to us. Zizi is not one to play mischievous tricks."

"But how did she get out?"

"How did Vernie's body get out?" asked Braye, gravely. "There's no chance for a human marauder this time."

"No," and Professor Hardwick looked over the great locks and bolts on the front doors, and examined the window catches.

Pennington Wise looked very serious.

"Don't talk any foolishness about spooks," he said, sternly; "I don't want to hear it. Zizi has been carried off by mortal hands, and if any harm has been done her it will go hard with the villain who is responsible!"

"Who could have done it—and why?" cried Eve.

"Those who know the most about it, are often the loudest in their lamentations," Wise returned and stalked off to his room.

Breakfast was eaten in a silence that seemed portentous of impending trouble. Pennington Wise was deep in thought and apparently had no knowledge of what he was eating nor any consciousness of the people about him.

During the meal a note was brought to him by a messenger from the village. He read it and slipped it in his pocket without a word.

After breakfast he requested the entire household, including the servants, to gather in the hall.

He addressed them in grave, earnest tones, without anger or undue excitement, saying, in part:

"I have made considerable progress in the investigations of the tragedies that have occurred in this house. I have learned much regarding the crimes and I think I have discovered who the guilty party is. I may say, in passing, that there is not, and has not been any supernatural influence at work. Any one who says that there has, is either blindly ignorant of or criminally implicated in the whole matter. The two deaths were vile and wicked murders and they are going to be avenged. The kidnapping of Zizi is the work of the same diabolical ingenuity that compassed the deaths of two innocent victims. A third death, that of my clever child assistant, was necessary to prevent discovery, hence Zizi's fate."

"Is she dead?" wailed Hester, "oh, Mr. Wise, is she dead?"

"I will tell you what happened to her," said Wise, quietly. "She was taken from her bed in the so-called haunted room, she was carried out of the house, and a bundle of bricks was tied to her, and she was thrown into the lake. That's what happened to Zizi."

Milly screamed hysterically, Norma Cameron cried softly and Eve Carnforth exclaimed, with blazing eyes, "I don't believe it! You are making that up! How can you know it? Why didn't you rescue her?"

The men uttered various exclamations of incredulity and horror, and the servants sat, aghast.

Pennington Wise surveyed rapidly one face after another, noting the expression of each, and sighing, as if disappointed.

"She is not dead," he said, suddenly, and watched again the telltale countenances.

"What!" cried Wynne Landon, "bricks tied to her, and thrown in the lake but not drowned! Who saved her life?"

"She herself," returned Wise, "didn't you, Zizi?"

And there she was, in the back of the hall, behind the group, every member of which turned to see her. Peterson was with her, and the two came forward.

Zizi was garbed in clothes that Mr. Peterson had lent her, and though too large, she had pinned up the plain black dress until it looked neither grotesque nor unbecoming.

"Yes, I'm here," she announced, "but only because a bag o' bones can't be sunk by a bag o' bricks! Your Shawled Woman,—only he didn't have his shawl over his head,—carried me off about as easy as he might have sneaked off a doll baby! Then,—shall I tell 'em all, Pen?"

"Yes, child, tell it all, just as it happened."

"Well, he stuffed a bale of cotton into my mouth, which same was soaked with chloroform, so, naturally I couldn't yell; likewise, I didn't know just where I was at for a few minutes."

"Who was he?" exclaimed Braye, "what did he look like?"

"Was it the skull face?" asked Eve.

"Nixy on the bone face!" returned Zizi, "he was a plain clothes man in civilian dress, with a black mask over his patrician features."

"Don't you know who it was?" and Eve's voice was intense and strained.

"Not positively," Zizi answered. "Well, he picked me up like I was a feather, and how he got out of the house I've no idea, but I felt a breeze of night air, and there was I by the bank of the lake, and there was he, busily engaged in tying a load of bricks to my ankles!"

"Did you scream?" asked the Professor, absorbed in the account.

"My dear man, how could I, with my mouth chock a block with a large and elegant bundle of gag? I was thankful that my wits were workin', let alone my lung power! Well, he tossed me in the nasty, black lake, and that's where he spilled the beans! For ground and lofty tumbling into lakes is my specialty. I'm the humble disciple of Miss Annette Kellerman, and not so awful humble, either! So, I held my breath under water long enough to wriggle my feet out of those ropes, the old stupid didn't know how to tie anything but a granny slip knot! and I scrambled out, just as my windpipe was beginning to go back on me."

"You make light of it, Zizi, but it was a narrow squeak," said Wise, looking at her gravely.

"You bet it was! If he'd had a softer rope, I'd been done for. It was the stiffness of that rope, and—well, the stiffness of my upper lip,—that rescued your little Ziz from a watery grave, and horrid dirty old water, too!"

Wise slipped his arm round the child, and told her to go on with the story.

"Then," she proceeded, "I squz out what wetness I could from my few scanty robes, in which I was bedecked, and I borrowed the long cloak, which friend Kidnapper had kindly wrapped me in."

"What kind of a cloak?" asked Eve.

"Nothing very smart," said Zizi, nonchalantly, "looked to me like an old fashioned waterproof,—the kind they wore, before raincoats came in. Only, it wasn't waterproof, not by several jugs full! But I wrung it out all I could, and then I tried to get in the house. But,—it was all locked up, and as it seemed a pity to disturb all you sound sleepers, I ran to the village and begged a lodging with my friend, Mr. Peterson. He and his wife were most kind, and put me in a nice dry, little bed, that had no tassels or ghosts attached to it. I sent Mr. Wise a note, as soon as I could, so he wouldn't worry."

"That was the note I received at the breakfast table," Wise informed them. "Now, you see, there is a real man at the bottom of the villainy going on up here. He desired to remove Zizi, lest she discover his crime, and I daresay, he planned to dispose of me also, if he could manage it. His seems to be a will that stops at nothing, that is ready to commit any crime or any number of crimes to save his own skin. Has anybody present any idea of the identity of this man? Any reason to suspect any one? Any light whatever to throw on the situation?"

"No!" declared Landon, "we have not! I speak for myself, and for all present, when I say we have no knowledge of a wretch answering to that description! Nor did I suppose that such existed! Can you track him down, Mr. Wise? Is your power sufficient to discover and deal death to this beast you describe?"

"I hope so," and Penny Wise carefully scrutinized the face of the speaker. "I think, Mr. Landon, that with Zizi's help, with the enlightenment her awful experience gives us, I can get the criminal and that in a short time."

"Good!" exclaimed Hardwick. "I am not vindictive, but I confess I never wanted anything more than to see brought to justice the man who could conceive and carry out such diabolical crimes!"

"Are you sure they are one and the same?" asked Braye, "I mean the man who killed Mr. Bruce and Vernie, and the one who carried off Miss Zizi?"

"Yes," said Wise, thoughtfully. "There are not two such, I should say. But the quest of one person is my immediate business. If I find there are others implicated, I shall get them, too. I am not more incensed over the attack on Zizi than on your two friends, but I don't deny it has given me an added wrong to avenge. But for the child's strong nerve, and clever quickness of action, she would now lie at the bottom of the lake where—"

He stopped abruptly.

"Go away, all of you," he said, in a low, strained voice. "I mean, go about your business, but leave me to myself for a time. Peterson, come in here."

He went into the Room with the Tassels. Peterson followed, and Zizi glided in beside them. The door closed and the group left in the hall looked at one another in perplexity and horror.

"I can't understand, Wynne," said Milly, "who took Zizi away?"

"I don't know, dear; what do you think, Professor?"

"I think in so many directions, that I'm sure none of them is right. Awful things suggest themselves to my mind, but I can't believe them, and I dismiss them, half thought out."

"'That's the way with me," sighed Braye. "It looks now as if there must be some one who gets in from outside the house, and who is responsible for all the inexplicable happenings. Of course, that would point to Stebbins, we must all admit that."

The servants had left the hall, so Braye permitted himself this freedom of speech.

"I don't say it's Stebbins," the Professor mused, "but I do think it's some one from outside. There may be a village inhabitant who is possessed of a homicidal mania, that's the theory that seems to me the only one possible. And we must assume, now, that there is a secret way to get in and out of the house."

"If so, that clever detective ought to find it," argued Braye.

"Perhaps he will," said Hardwick, "also, perhaps he has. He doesn't tell all he knows. Now, this is certain. All here present are, I am thankful to say, free from any breath of suspicion. For last night, you, Braye, and the detective and I all slept with our doors open, and none of us could have left our rooms without being observed by the others. The same is true of the ladies, and of course, Mrs. Landon can vouch for her husband."

"Don't talk that way," said Norma, with a shudder. "You know none of us could be suspected."

"Not by ourselves," agreed the Professor; "nor by each other, of course. But by an outsider, or by the servants, or by the detectives,—it is indeed a good thing to have matters arranged as they are. I feel a decided satisfaction in knowing that no unjust suspicion can attach itself to any one of our party."

"That's so," and Braye nodded. "But it doesn't get us any nearer to the real criminal. I incline to the Professor's idea of a man of homicidal mania, in the village. They say, that's a real disease, and that such people are diabolically clever and cunning in carrying out their criminal impulses."

"But how could such a man get in?" asked Eve, her eyes wide with wonder.

"We don't know," said Braye, "but there must be a secret entrance. Why, Stebbins as good as admitted there was, but he wouldn't tell where it was. However, it's unimportant, how he got in, if he did get in."

"Do you mean that some such person acted the ghost,—and—all that?" said Norma, dubiously.

"But, if so, how could he kill Mr. Bruce and Vernie? Oh, it's too ridiculous! Those two deaths were not occasioned by any crazy man from East Dryden! It's impossible."

"Come out for a little stroll, Norma," said Braye to her, seeing how nervously excited the girl was. "A breath of fresh air will do you good, and we can do nothing here."

They went out into the pleasant August sunshine, and strolled toward the lake.

"Not that way," begged Norma. "It's too horrible. Oh, Rudolph, who do you suppose tried to drown that poor little Zizi?"

"Nobody, Norma. She made up that yarn."

"Oh, no, Rudolph, I don't think so!"

"Yes, she did. That Wise is trying to get at his discoveries in the theatrical fashion all detectives love to use, and that movie actress is part of his stock in trade. She fell in the lake, all right, I daresay, but the tale about the bogey man is fictitious, be sure of that."

"But how did she get out of the house, and leave all the doors locked behind her?"

"Perhaps, as the Professor suggested, Wise knows of the secret entrance, if there is one, and of course, Zizi does too. Or, that little monkey could have scrambled down from the second story window, she's as agile as a cat! Anyway, Norma, she wasn't pitched in the lake by the same villain that did for Uncle Gif and Vernie."

"Who could that have been?"

"Who, indeed?"

"Rudolph, tell me one thing,—please be frank; do you think any one we know–is,—is responsible for those deaths?"

Braye turned a pained look at her. "Don't ask such questions, dear," he said. "I can't answer you,—I don't want to answer."

"I am answered," said Norma, sadly. "I know you share the—the fear, I won't call it a suspicion,—that Eve and I do. And—Rudolph, Milly fears it, too. She won't say so, of course, but I know by the way she looks at Wynne, when she thinks no one notices. And she's so afraid Mr. Wise will look in that direction. Oh, Rudolph, must we let that detective go on,—no matter what he—exposes?"

"Landon got him up here," said Braye, "no, the Professor really heard of him first, but Landon urged his coming."

"Milly didn't. Could Wynne have been prompted by— by bravado?"

"I don't know, dear. Please don't talk of it, Norma. It seems—"

"I know, it seems disloyal to Wynne for us even to hint at such a thing. But if we could help him—"

"How?"

"Oh, I don't know. I suppose we oughtn't to condone,— and, too, Rudolph, if this should remain undiscovered, should be all hushed up, you know, and if nobody should really accuse—you know who—wouldn't *your* life be in danger?"

"Hush, Norma, I won't listen to such talk! Has Eve put you up to all this?"

"She and I have talked it over, yes. She is so anxious for you."

"For me?"

"Yes; you know Eve—cares a great deal for you."

"Hush, dear, you're not yourself to day. And I don't wonder. The awful times we're going through are enough to upset your nerves. But never speak of Eve Carnforth and me in that tone! You know, Norma, I love you and you only. I want you for my own, my darling, and when we get away from these awful scenes, I shall woo and win you!"

CHAPTER 17: STEBBINS OWNS UP

"NOW, Mr. Stebbins, you'd better speak out in meetin' and tell all you know. Tell your Auntie Zizi jes' how naughty you was, and how you managed it. C'mon, now,—'pit it all out!"

Zizi sat on the edge of a chair in Elijah Stebbins' office, and leaned toward him, her eerie little face enticingly near his, and her smile such as would charm the birds off the trees.

Stebbins looked at her, and shifted uneasily in his chair.

"I didn't do nothin' wrong," he began, "I played a silly trick or two, but it was only in fun. When I see they took it seriously, I quit."

"Yes, I know all that," and the impatient visitor shook a prompting little forefinger at him. "I know everything you said and did to scare those people into fits, and when they wouldn't scare, but just lapped up your spook rackets, you quit, as you say, and then,—they took up the business themselves."

"You sure of that?"

"I am,—certain. Also, I know who did it. What I'm after is to find out a few missing ways and means. Now, you *were* a tricksy Puck, weren't you, when you moved the old battered candlestick that first night? And it did no harm, that I admit. It roused their curiosity, and started the spook ball rolling. Then, as a ghost, you appeared to Mr. Bruce, didn't you?"

"Well, I—did," Stebbins grudgingly confessed, forced by the compelling black eyes, "I just wrop a shawl over my head, and spooked in. But nobody believed his yarn about it."

"No; they thought Mr. Bruce made up the story, because he had said he would trick them if he could."

"Yep, I know that," agreed Stebbins, eagerly. "Then once again, I played spook, and that time, Miss Carnforth was a sleepin' in that ha'nted room. You see, I expected it would be one o' the men, and when I see a woman—"

"You were more scared than she was!" Zizi leaned eagerly forward, almost spilling off her chair, in her interested attention.

"I believe I was," said Stebbins, solemnly. "Anyways, I went out, vowin' never to do any more spook work,—and I never did."

"All that tallies with my discoveries so far," Zizi nodded, "now what I'm after, is the way you got in."

"That's a secret," and Stebbins squirmed uneasily.

"A secret entrance, you mean?"

"Yes 'm. And how to get into it is a secret that has been known only to the owner of that house, for generations,—ever since it was built. Whenever anybody bought it or inherited it, he was told the secret entrance, and sworn never to tell of it."

"But, look here, Mr. Stebbins, your entrance to that house, or whatever it is, was seen by somebody. That somebody used it afterward, and played ghost, and committed crime, and even stole the body of that poor little girl away. Also, some one carried me,–*me!* if you please, out by that secret passage, and tried to drown me! Now, do you think it is your duty to remain silent, because of that old oath of secrecy?"

Zizi had risen and stood over him like a small but terrifying avenging angel. If she had brandished a flaming sword, it could not have impressed Eli Stebbins more than her burning black eyes' glance. Her long, thin arms were outspread, her slim body poised on tiptoe and her accusing, condemning face was white and strained in its earnestness.

"No, ma'am, I don't!" and Stebbins rose, too. "Come with me, Miss; I'll go with you and I'll show you that secret entrance, nobody could ever find it alone, and I'll own up to all I did, wrong or right. I'm no murderer, and I'll not put a straw in the way of findin' out who is."

In triumph, Zizi entered the hall of Black Aspens, leading her captive. Though it must be admitted Stebbins came willingly.

"This here's my house," he said, with an air of importance, "and so far's I'm responsible for queer goin's on, I'll confess. And after that, you, Mr. Detective, can find out who carried on the hocus pocus."

"Thank you, Mr. Stebbins," said Pennington Wise, gravely. "Suppose we ask all the members of the household to be present at your revelations."

"Not the Thorpes, or them servant maids, if you please. They ain't none of 'em implicated, and why let 'em know what's goin' on?"

"That's right," said Zizi. "Whatever we learn may not be entirely given to the public. Just call the rest of the party, Pen."

As it happened, the men were all in the hall talking with Wise when Stebbins arrived, so Zizi went in search of the women. They were congregated in Milly's room, and as they came downstairs, the detective noted their expressions, a favourite method with him of gaining information.

Milly's round little face was so red and swollen with weeping, that it excited only compassion in any observer. Norma, too, was sad and frightened looking, but Eve was in a defiant mood, and her scarlet lips were curved in a disdainful smile.

"As we're all at one in our search for the criminal," Wise began, tactfully, "I think it best that we should hear, all together, Mr. Stebbins' explanation of how this house may be entered from outside, though apparently locked and bolted against intrusion."

"I should think, Mr. Wise," said Eve, scornfully, "that if there were such a possibility, your detective genius ought to have discovered it."

"He couldn't," said Stebbins, simply. "It ain't a means that any one could discover."

"Then how did the criminal find it out?" demanded Eve.

"He must have seen me come in by it," Stebbins replied. "Nobody could ever suspect the real way."

"Oh, come now," said Zizi, "Mr. Wise does know. He is not at all vain glorious, or he would tell you himself. But he prefers to let Mr. Stebbins tell."

"Is that so, Mr. Wise?" asked Professor Hardwick, eagerly. "If you have discovered the secret entrance, I wish you would say so. I feel chagrined that my own reasoning powers have given me no hint."

"I have satisfied myself of the means and the location of the entrance," Wise returned, "but I have not examined the place definitely enough to find the hidden spring that must be there."

"You know that much!" cried Stebbins, in amazement.

"Yes, largely by elimination. There are no hollow walls, no false locks, no sliding panels,—it seems to me there is no logical hidden entrance, but through one of those columns," and he pointed to the great bronze columns that flanked the doorway.

"By golly!" and Stebbins stared at the speaker. "You've hit it, sir!"

"I could, of course, find the secret spring, which must be concealed in the ornamentation," Wise went on, "but I've hesitated to draw attention to the columns by working at them. Suppose we let Mr. Stebbins tell us, and not try to find what we know must be cleverly concealed."

"But wait a minute," pleaded Hardwick. "I'm terribly interested in this proof of Mr. Wise's perspicacity. You needn't touch the column, but tell us your theory of its use. Is there a sliding opening in the solid bronze?"

"I think not," and Wise smiled. "I may be all wrong, I really haven't looked closely, but my belief it that one or both of those great columns, which, as you see, are half in and half out of the hall, must swing round, revolve, you know,—and so open a way out."

"Exactly right!" and Stebbins sprang toward the column that was on the side of the hall toward the Room with the Tassels. "That's the secret. Nobody ever so much as dreamed of it before! See, you merely press this acorn in this bronze oak wreath, half way up, press it pretty hard, and the column swings round."

They crowded closer to see, and learned that the column was made in two half sections, one in the hall and one outside. These, again, were divided horizontally, about seven feet above the floor, and the joint concealed by a decorative wreath of bronze oak boughs.

The column was hollow, and one half the shaft revolved within the other, which, in turn, revolved over the first, so that by successive movements of the two, one could pass right through the vestibule wall, and close the opening after him, leaving no trace of his entry or exit. The vestibule wall, of mahogany, concealed the longitudinal joint in the column when closed. The doors were hinged to this wooden wall, and were opened and closed, and locked, quite independently of the columns. Owing to perfectly adjusted ball bearings, and a thoroughly oiled condition, the mechanism worked easily and soundlessly.

"The whole contraption was brought from Italy," Stebbins informed them, "by the original Montgomery. I don't think he ever used it for any wrong doings, though they do say, soldiers was smuggled through in war times, and contraband smuggling went on, too. But those is only rumours and probably exaggerated."

"You exaggerated the ghost stories, too, didn't you, Mr. Stebbins?" asked Wise.

"I didn't need to, sir. Those yarns of the Shawled Woman, have been told and retold so many years now, they've grown way beyond their first facts, if there ever was any truth to 'em. This here column, only one of 'em revolves,—has always been kept secret, but when the little witch child made me see it was my duty to tell of it, tell of it I did. Now, sir, go ahead and find who committed them dastardly murders and I'll consider I did right to break my oath of secrecy."

"No one will blame you for it," said Professor Hardwick, who was still experimenting with the revolving column. "This is a marvellous piece of workmanship, Landon. I never saw such before."

Pennington Wise was covertly watching all the faces as the various ones peered into the opening left when the column was turned. He stood on guard, too, and when Eve curiously bent down to open a long box, which stood up on end, against the inside of the bronze cylinder, he reached ahead of her.

"Yes," he said, consentingly, "let us see what is in here."

In full view of all, he opened the long box, such a box as long stemmed roses might have been packed in, and took from it a voluminous cloak of thin white material, a flimsy, white shawl, and a mask that represented a skull.

"The paraphernalia of the Shawled Woman," the detective said, exhibiting the things, "your property, Mr. Stebbins?"

"Yes, they are," and the man looked shame faced, but determined. "I made all my plans, before the folks came up here, to ha'nt the Room with the Tassels. I meant no harm, I vow. I thought they was a silly set of society folks, who believed in spooks, and I thought I'd give 'em what they come for. I bought the mask at a fancy shop in town, and the thin stuff too. The shawl is one my wife used to have. I own up to all my doin's, because while they was foolish, and maybe mean, they wasn't criminal. Now, if so be's somebody saw me go in and out, and used those ghost clo'es, which it seems they must have done, I'll help all I can to fasten the guilt where it belongs."

"I, too," declared Rudolph Braye. "It certainly looks as if some one had seen Mr. Stebbins enter the house secretly, and watching, saw him leave. Then, this night prowler tried the game himself."

"Yes, sir," replied Stebbins. "Just the same sort of spring, inside and out. Anybody seein' me go through, either way, could easily work out the secret. But, not knowing of it, nobody'd ever suspect."

"Of course not," agreed Braye. "Now, we have a start, let us get to work on the more serious aspect of the affair. For, while this revelation explains the entrance of some midnight marauder, with intent to frighten us, it doesn't do much toward lessening the mystery of those two deaths."

"You're sure, Mr. Stebbins," and Eve turned glittering eyes on him, "that you never 'haunted' after that night when you appeared to me! You know a ghost appeared to Vernie after that. Can we believe that was not the work of the same malignant—"

"Malignant is not the word to apply to Mr. Stebbins," Pennington Wise interrupted her, "and it is up to us,—to me, to find who took his place as haunter of this house. Also, who it was that removed the body of Vernie Reid, doubtless through the revolving column, and—who kidnapped and tried to drown Zizi."

"Those are secondary problems," said Braye, thoughtfully gazing at the detective. "But they must be solved, too, of course. What I'm more anxious about, however, is to learn how any one could compass the murders,—if murders they were."

"Of course they were," said Hardwick. "Now that I know as much as I do know, I'm sure we'll learn all. Mr. Wise, I'm of a detective bent, myself, and you may count on me to help you all I can. You needn't laugh—"

"My dear Professor Hardwick, I assure you I've no thought of laughing, or of belittling the help you offer. I'm truly glad of your assistance and it is my habit to be frank with my clients, so we need have no reservations, on either side. The assurance we have received that an intruder could and did enter the house, gives us new directions in which to look and new theories to pursue. I'm sure you will all agree with me that the body of Miss Reid was carried out through the secret column, and not removed by supernatural means."

"Without doubt," said Rudolph Braye, but Eve Carn forth looked a denial.

"I can't agree," she said, "that the discovery of a secret entrance disproves all possibility of the presence of supernatural agencies. I think no human intruder can be held responsible for all we have been through. How do you account for two deaths occurring at the very moment they were foretold?"

Her question was evidently addressed to Wise, and he replied, "I think, Miss Carnforth, that those two deaths were murders, cleverly accomplished by human wills, and it is my immediate duty to prove this. Therefore, I am now going to endeavour to recover the missing body of the unfortunate girl who was killed."

"What! Vernie's body!" and Eve gasped.

"Yes. And not wishing to do anything to which you may not all agree, I announce frankly that I am going to have the lake dragged."

"The lake!" cried Wynne Landon, "why, man, it is miles long!"

"But I think that the same person who tried to drown Zizi is responsible for the disappearance of Miss Reid's body, and I feel sure that if we look in that same part of the lake we will find what we are after."

"Incredible!" exclaimed Landon. "You will only waste your time!"

Wise looked closely at the face of the speaker, and then turned quickly to observe another face.

"At any rate, it can do no harm to try," he said, finally.

"Not at all," said Braye; "go ahead. But even the recovery of Vernie's body, will get us no nearer to her murderer. I wish I had been here at the time of those deaths. While I cannot feel I should have been of any help, I do think I could have noticed something or formed some opinion or conclusion from the circumstances."

"No, Rudolph," said the Professor. "There was nothing to be seen or deduced from anything that happened at that time. I was nearest to Mr. Bruce, Miss Carnforth was nearest to Vernie. Neither of us saw anything suspicious or of unexplainable intent."

"And yet Mr. Bruce was poisoned," said Wise, glancing from one face to another. "And I feel positive Miss Reid was also poisoned. She must have been. What else could have killed her, like that?"

"True enough," and Braye nodded his head. "But do you think an examination of her body, after all this time, could prove that?"

"Whether it could or not," said Wise, "we want to recover the body if possible. My theory is that it must have been thrown in the lake. If it was taken away through the revolving column, what else could have been done with it? To bury it would have been to risk discovery. And Zizi's experience—"

"Are you sure, Mr. Wise, that Zizi's experience was truthfully related? May she not have been hysterically nervous, and imagined the whole thing? I've heard of such cases."

"Who put you up to that idea, Miss Carnforth?" said Wise, very quietly, and Eve flushed and turned aside, remaining silent.

Pennington Wise's theory proved the true one.

The men employed to drag the lake at Black Aspens succeeded in finding the body of Vernie Reid. A bag of bricks had been tied to the ankles, in the same manner as described by Zizi, and the little form had been sunk in almost the same place that Zizi had been flung into the water.

Reverent hands carried the body to the house, and later it was examined by a skilled physician from New York City.

He reported that death had ensued upon the girl's arm being scratched with some sharp implement, which had been previously dipped in a powerful poison.

As this was the same physician who had passed the final judgment on the cause of Mr. Bruce's death, his report was listened to with confidence and belief.

"You must know," he said, to the awed group, "that about last March, a plot was formed against some high officials in England. These diabolical plans included the use of extremely poisonous drugs. By a most culpable oversight the names and descriptions of these poisons crept into the public press, and since then, several attempts at their use have been made, mostly, I am glad to say, without result.

"But, it is clear to me, that the murderer of these two people, Mr. Bruce, and the child, Vernie Reid, used the poisons I have told you of."

"I read about them," said Pennington Wise. "They included a rare drug only to be obtained from South America."

"That was the statement," said the doctor, "but I'm credibly informed there is a supply secretly hoarded in this country. However that may be, I am convinced that was the means used in Miss Reid's case. This poison must be introduced under the skin, by means of a cut or scratch, whereupon, the effect is instantaneously fatal. Twenty seconds is said to be the extreme length of time for life to remain in a body after the introduction of the venom. There is a distinct scratch on Miss Reid's upper right arm, so inflamed and poisoned as to leave no doubt in the matter."

"That's why the body was removed," said the Professor, "lest that scratch be discovered."

"Yes," agreed Wise, "and the other victim, Mr. Bruce, was killed by having the poison introduced into his stomach."

"That was a different poison," said the doctor. "That was strychnine hydrochlorate, which acts with equal speed. The evidential point is, that these two poisons were both plotted to be used in the case I mentioned in England, which, however, was foiled before it was actually attempted. The grave wrong, was the account in the newspapers, which was so circumstantial and definite as to give information to whoever cared to use it. Can any one doubt that the villain in this case, read the article I speak of, which was in several of our American papers, and made use of his ill gotten directions to achieve his purpose?"

"How did it get into Mr. Bruce's stomach?" demanded Braye.

"It was secretly placed in his tea or in the cake he was eating," declared the doctor. "Don't ask me how,—or who did it. That is not my province. But whoever could plan these fearsome deeds, could find an ingenious method of carrying out his plans,—of that I'm sure."

"I wish I'd been present," said Braye, again, as he sighed deeply.

CHAPTER 18: ANOTHER CONFESSION

PENNINGTON WISE and Zizi sat in the hall talking. It was part of Wise's policy never to hold secret conclaves with his little assistant, for, he said that the people who employed him were entitled to all his suspicions or deductions as they took shape and grew in his mind. Professor Hardwick joined them as Wise was saying, "What first turned your attention to the Room with the Tassels, Ziz? Why did you move into that room to sleep?"

"Because the lock was oiled," Zizi replied, her black eyes glistening. "The first time I got a chance I looked at all the locks in the house, and only two were freshly oiled, and they had been well looked after,—I can tell you."

"What did that prove to you?" Hardwick asked.

"That somebody was haunting the Room with the Tassels who had to open the door to get in. No ghost would need to turn a knob—and open the door. They splash right through walls or anything, or they ought to, if they know their business! But this lock, as well as the knob, was oiled, and, as you know, the door was opened though locked on the inside. Clever fingers can turn a key from the other side, if they have a certain implement, used by burglars. Also, if the key was not in the door, clever people could provide a duplicate key. But these things are not necessary for ghosts. They just glide in serenely, not even thinking about keys or doors."

"You're right, child," and Wise nodded approvingly at her. "Now, what other door had its lock oiled?"

"Not only the lock, but the hinges of one of the bedroom doors were carefully oiled. You know which one, Penny."

"I do, Zizi. Have you no suspicion, Professor?"

"I'd rather not say. As a friend of all the people in our party, I simply can't bring myself to mention the name of any one of them, and, yet if one of us is a criminal, it is the duty of the others to see justice done."

"Well, it must soon come out, anyway. It is Mr. Tracy's door, isn't it, Zizi?"

"Yes."

"Bless my soul!" cried the Professor, "Tracy! Why, he's a minister!"

"No," and Penny Wise shook his head, "Mr. Tracy is not a minister and never was. On the contrary, he's about as far removed from piety of any sort, as any man on God's green earth!"

"What are you saying?" cried Eve Carnforth, coming swiftly toward them. "Mr. Tracy not a minister!"

"No;" repeated Wise, "John Tracy is a notorious criminal, known as Smug Johnny by his friends, and also by the police. I have just had returns from some inquiries I sent to Chicago, and I learn that this double dyed villain is wanted on several counts, but never before has he been accused of murder."

"And did he kill Mr. Bruce and Vernie?" cried Eve, her hands clenched in excitement and her long eyes narrowed with fear.

"He did, I am positive. We have yet to prove it, but I have evidence enough "

"Where is he?" said Hardwick, abruptly.

"Under strict surveillance," returned Wise. "My men are at his heels day and night. He can't get away."

"He stole me," said Zizi; "you see I had my eye on him, 'cause of his oiled door. Then when he came, I thought he was only going to scare me, but he stuffed that old chloroform in my mouth so quick, I couldn't even yell out. If I hadn't had some experience in swimming pools and movie thrillers, I'd been down at the bottom of that horrid old lake this minute!"

"But I can't understand," and Eve looked puzzled; "why would Mr. Tracy kill those people, and how did he do it? Mr. Wise, you're crazy! It's an impossible theory!"

Others had gathered in the hall, now, and Pennington Wise told them all of his recent advices from Chicago, that proved the supposed clergyman a fraud and a villain.

Milly showed the greatest relief. "Oh," she cried, "I'm glad you've found out who it was, anyway! But it doesn't seem as if Mr. Tracy could be a bad man—are you sure, Mr. Wise?"

"Yes, Mrs. Landon, there is no doubt at all. Now, let us reconstruct the scene of those two deaths. Where was Mr. Tracy sitting?"

"Right here, where I am now," said Norma, thinking back. "Vernie was over there, near the front door. Mr. Bruce was across the hall by Professor Hardwick, and Eve was in the middle of the room by the tea table."

"Will you be so kind, Miss Carnforth, as to think very carefully," said Wise, "and see if you recollect Mr. Tracy's presence near you as you were fixing the various cups of tea. Did he have the slightest opportunity to add anything to the cup that was afterward handed to Mr. Bruce?"

Excited, almost hysterical, Eve obeyed the detective's command, and said, after a moment's thought, "Yes, he did. I remember he passed near me, and Vernie stood at my side also. They had a bit of good natured banter as to which should take the cup I had just poured out, and Vernie won, and she laughingly carried it to Mr. Bruce. I remember it distinctly."

"Then, doubtless, at that moment, Tracy dropped the small amount of poison necessary in the cup, sure that it would be given to Mr. Bruce. Had Vernie given it to any one else, he would have intercepted it. He is a man of suave manners, you know."

"Yes," said Norma, "particularly so, and very graceful about any social matters. He always assisted in passing the tea things."

"Go on," said Penny Wise; "what happened as Mr. Bruce took his first sip of tea?"

"He changed countenance at once," said Hardwick. "I was talking to him, and a queer pallor came over his face and then it turned fiery red. He dropped his cup and—"

"One moment," said Wise; "what became of that broken cup?"

"I've no idea," said the Professor, helplessly looking about him.

"I wasn't home," began Milly, "Mr. Braye and I had gone to East Dryden—"

"The tray was taken out as usual," interposed Eve, but Norma said, quietly, "I picked up the broken bits and laid them on the tray."

"Call in the servant who took away that tray," said Wise, shortly.

Old Thorpe was called in, and told his story.

"I came in for the tray," he said, and seein'—what I did see—I was fair knocked out. I did as usual, and picked up the tray to carry it to the kitchen. Mr. Tracy was by the tray at the time, and he was pourin' hot water into the teacups. I don't think the man knew what he was about,—none of us did, and small wonder!"

Thorpe knew nothing of the recent developments regarding Tracy, and Wise pursued: "Do you remember whether Mr. Tracy poured hot water over the broken cup?"

"That's just what he was doin', sir, that's why I thought he didn't rightly know what he was about."

"You may go, Thorpe," said Wise.

"You see," he continued after the old man had gone, "Tracy poured boiling hot water from the afternoon teakettle over the broken cup, that all evidence of poison might be removed, if the bits of china were examined. I've not heard of that being done, however, but a guilty conscience would naturally fear it. That little incident shows the astuteness of his criminal mind."

"It does!" cried Professor Hardwick. "What a depraved, a demoniacal nature must be his! Where did he come from? Who introduced him to our party ?"

"I did," said Rudolph Braye. "I had, of course, no suspicion of his real nature. I met Tracy on the train, travelling from Chicago to New York, about a year ago. He was a pleasant smoking-room companion, and I've seen him several times since, in New York. I had no reason to think him other than what he represented himself, a clergyman, with a church in Chicago. He impressed me as a fine, congenial sort, and when Mrs. Landon asked me to suggest another member for our house party, I thought of him at once. His cloth seemed to me to be his adequate credentials and, in fact, I never gave a thought to his possible duplicity! Nor can I reconcile the facts, even yet. How do you know these things, Mr. Wise? Are you not romancing a little?"

"No, Mr. Braye, I am not even surmising. What I have stated is true, because there is no other possible deduction from the facts I have learned. I have identified the man Tracy who was here with you as the notorious Smug Johnny of Chicago. Do you need further knowledge of him to believe that he is the criminal in this case, rather than one of your own immediate circle?"

"No," and Milly shuddered; "it is bad enough that it should have been Mr. Tracy, but far better than to suspect one of us here."

"Furthermore," continued Wise, "let us look into the details of the death of Vernie Reid. Who can give me the exact facts as noticed?"

"I," said Eve Carnforth; "and, now, as I look back, I see it all in a different light! I was looking at Mr. Bruce, as everybody was, startled by the sound of crashing china, and I heard Mr. Tracy say, 'Vernie, child! What is the matter?' or some such words. Then he ran quickly to her side and held her up in his arms, while I ran to them and helped him to lay her on the sofa."

"See?" said Wise; "at the moment Tracy sprang toward the girl she was unharmed, and as he put his arm round her, he scratched her arm with a sharp pointed instrument, which had been dipped in the awful poison that we have learned of. It is said to be similar to that with which the barbarians of South America tip their arrows. But the least scratch is instantly fatal, and proved so in Vernie's case. The instrument he used, we have reason to think, was a steel pen."

"Why do you think that?" asked Professor Hardwick.

"Because Zizi found a few new ones in Tracy's room, that had not been used for writing purposes. There were five in a small paper parcel. We have found that he bought these at a shop in the village, buying six at the time. This is merely a shred of evidence, but the fact that Zizi found the pens became known to Mr. Tracy, in fact he caught her searching his room. It was this that made him try to do away with the child."

"Tracy? Do away with Zizi!" exclaimed Braye. "Why, he was gone away from here, then."

"No. He had left the house, but he was lurking about, and after all had retired that night, he came through the revolving column, and kidnapped Zizi, and threw her into the lake,—as he had previously thrown in the body of Vernie Reid. That, he did, lest the scratch on her arm be discovered by the doctors, and he be suspected."

"Then it was Tracy who discovered the secret of the revolving column," said Braye, thoughtfully. "You take a great deal for granted, Mr. Wise."

"I take nothing for granted, save what the facts prove, Mr. Braye. That Tracy used the revolving column is positive. Do you not all remember the night when Professor Hardwick saw the apparition of the Shawled Woman? On that night Mr. Tracy was supposed to be in Boston. As a matter of fact, he was not, he had left the house, saying he was going to Boston but he remained in hiding near the house, played ghost, and then went on his way."

"I was in New York that night," said Braye, musingly. "But, look here, Mr. Wise, one afternoon, about dusk, Miss Cameron and I distinctly saw the apparition of the Shawled Woman in the Room with the Tassels when we ourselves were out of doors. We saw it through the window,—don't you remember, Norma?"

"I do,— "

"Then that was Mr. Tracy's doings also," declared Wise. "How simple for him to get the paraphernalia from the column, where it was always in readiness, make his appearance to frighten you two, and then return the shawl and so forth before you could enter and catch him."

"It would have been possible," agreed Braye, and then Hardwick began.

"There were many other strange things to be accounted for, such as meanings and rustlings in the morning at four o'clock, and also occasional odours of prussic acid, without apparent reason."

"Lay them all to Tracy," said Wise, "you won't be far out. Now, who was running that Ouija board the night it said the two people would die at four o'clock?"

"Vernie and Mr. Tracy," said Norma, "but when it said that, Mr. Tracy took his hands off and said he would have no more to do with it. He said he believed Vernie pushed it to those letters."

"He was a good actor," said Wise, looking grave and sighing; "he fooled you all, it would seem."

"He certainly fooled me, good and plenty," said Braye, angrily. "You say you have him in custody, Mr. Wise?"

"I did not say that, but I have him under such surveillance that he cannot get away. There are some other matters to be discussed. Granting Tracy's guilt, what do you ascribe as a motive?"

There was a profound silence. What could have been the motive for a perfect stranger to kill with deliberation two people who had never injured him in any way, and from whose death he could expect no pecuniary advantage?

"Look here," said Wynne Landon, suddenly, "Mr. Tracy went away from here because the spectre appeared to him. How do you account for that?"

"Mr. Tracy *said* so," returned Wise, "but that story of his ghostly vision was made up out of the whole cloth,— which was all of the 'cloth' with which he ever had to do."

"He made up that yarn, then, as an excuse to get away?" said Hardwick.

"He did just that," replied Wise. "But what has any one to suggest as Mr. Tracy's motive for the crimes he committed?"

"Plain homicidal mania," offered Hardwick, at last, as no one else spoke.

"No," said Wise, "John Tracy is not of that type. Such people are abnormal, they have special physical characteristics, and they are easily recognized, once suspicion is attached to them. Tracy is a quiet, even debonair character, he is even tempered, gentle mannered and though deeply clever he hides it under a mask of kindliness and consideration. Victims of what is called homicidal mania are not at all like this. They are difficult to get along with, they do queer, inexplicable things, and most of all, they show in their faces the traits that lead them to their villainous deeds. You all know Tracy is not of this type. Therefore you must look further for his motive."

"Did he receive any bequest from Mr. Bruce's will?" asked Hardwick, wonderingly.

"Certainly not," asserted Landon. "He didn't know Mr. Bruce until we came up here, and that would have been no motive for his killing Vernie. Nor can there be any personal motive, Mr. Wise, for that. Shall we not have to ascribe it to some form of degeneracy, whether that seems plausible or not?"

"No," decreed Wise, looking sternly from one to another. "No; John Tracy's motive for those two inhuman murders was the motive that is oftenest the reason for murder—money lust!"

Eve Carnforth gave a scream and buried her face in her hands.

Milly Landon turned white and swayed as if about to faint, but her husband caught her in his arms and supported her.

"What can he mean?" said Norma, turning to Braye, "how could Mr. Tracy have done it for money? Who would give him money?"

"Hush, Norma," said Braye, in a low voice, and Norma remembered it was the same tone he had used, when she had before asked questions of him. She had thought over his words on that occasion, and had concluded he meant she must not say anything that seemed to throw suspicion toward Wynne Landon. She looked at the sobbing Milly, and the pained, strained face of Wynne, who was trying to soothe her, and then Norma turned to Eve.

Eve was using all her will power to preserve her poise, but Norma saw at once that she was having difficulty to do so. In kindness of heart, Norma went over to the suffering girl.

"Come with me, Eve," she said, softly, "let us go off by ourselves for a while."

"Yes, do," said Penny Wise, looking kindly at the two girls. "Zizi, perhaps you can be of use."

Zizi followed the other two, and they went to Eve's room. With all the deftness of a nurse, Zizi found some aromatic cologne, and a fresh hand kerchief, and in a moment was bathing Eve's temples, with a gentle, soothing touch.

"What a funny little piece you are!" said Eve, looking at the small sympathetic face, and speaking in a preoccupied way.

"Yes," acquiesced Zizi, while Norma sat by, lost in her own thoughts.

"Tell me," said Eve, suddenly roused to energy. "Tell me, Zizi,—you know as much as Mr. Wise does,—tell me, who paid Tracy money?"

"What!" cried Norma, "Eve, hush! don't say such things. If anybody did, we don't want to know it!"

"We'll have to know it," said Eve, simply, "and, Norma,—"

But Norma interrupted her; "No, Eve, we don't have to, at least, we don't have to ask about it, or inquire into it. The detective will do that."

"You'll soon have to know," said Zizi, quietly; "indeed you know now, don't you, Miss Camforth?"

"I asked you!" cried Eve, hysterical again. "Tell me, tell me at once, girl!"

But Zizi shook her head, and continued to bathe Eve's brow. "Try to be calm," she whispered, "there will be much for you to bear, and you must be brave to bear it."

Eve looked at her wonderingly, and seeing deep compassion in the black eyes, she ceased questioning and closed her own eyes.

After a few moments, she opened her eyes and rose from her couch. "Thank you, Zizi," she said, "I am all right now. I am going back to join the others. Will you come, Norma?"

Dazedly, as one in a dream, Norma rose, and the three went down stairs. Apparently little had been said of importance since they left. There was a tense silence, and Pennington Wise said, "I find I must speak out and tell you the truth. I had hoped for a confession but I see no signs of it.

"I was not, strictly speaking, employed by any one of you. I asked to be allowed to investigate this case because it seemed to me the most remark able one I had ever heard of. I wrote to Professor Hardvvick for information concerning it, and finally I arranged to come up here. I brought Zizi, because she is invaluable to me in collecting evidence. Her quick wit, and her dainty personality can compass effects that I can not. I feel, therefore, that it is to Professor Hard wick that I should make my direct report. But as you are all interested, I will ask any of you who choose to do so, to remain and listen. The others may be excused."

"Of course, we'll all stay!" exclaimed Landon.

"We're all quite as much interested as Professor Hardwick can possibly be. More so, indeed, for the victims of the crime are not relatives of his."

"Very well," returned Wise, "stay, then, all of you. The story is not a long one, though it is a deeply sad one. John Tracy was hired,—basely hired, to commit those two murders. The man who hired him is, of course, the greater criminal, though his hands are unstained with actual blood. The man who hired the assassin, is, naturally, the man who desired the large fortune of Gifford Bruce, and who realized that unless two people were removed from earth he could not inherit. Need I say more?"

"You need not," said Rudolph Braye. "I confess. The plan was Tracy's, the suggestion was his. He tempted me, by telling me that he had read of a plan by which people could be put to death and leave no possible trace. He said that I would eventually inherit the fortune, and that I ought to have it while I was young enough to enjoy it. He said he would do the deed and I need know nothing about it, nor be present at the time. I am not shifting the blame, I am merely telling you the facts."

Braye spoke in a monotone, his eyes on the floor, his hands nervously twitching.

"A hundred times I regretted our plans, a hundred times I begged Tracy to give up the project, but he held me to it, and said if I petered out he would tell the whole story.

"When the plan for coming up here was started, Tracy made me get him invited saying it was an ideal opportunity. I didn't think he would really carry out his intentions, and as the ghost seemed really to appear, I watched to discover the means. I did see Stebbins enter through the revolving column and had no difficulty in discovering how it worked. I showed this to Tracy,—he made me do so,—and when I went to New York, he played ghost and appeared to little Vernie.

"Again and again I plead with him to give up the fearful scheme but he refused to do so. The day I went to East Dryden with Milly I had no idea that he intended to do the deed, but—he did. I had promised him half the fortune, and he had declared that there could be no suspicion of either of us,—he said, if there were any suspicion it would be directed toward Wynne. I make no excuses, I voice no cry for forgiveness or for leniency, but I hereby pay the penalty."

Braye swallowed what was evidently a portion of the same poison that had killed Gifford Bruce, and in less than a minute he was a dead man.

John Tracy was arrested and received his just deserts.

Wynne Landon inherited the fortune, and though it had painful associations, he and Milly went away from Black Aspens never to return and in time lived down the sad and awful memories.

"You see, Penny," Zizi summed up, "a criminal always slips up on some minor count. If the Tracy person hadn't oiled his door and the door of that haunted room so carefully, or if he'd had the wit to oil some other doors too, we might have overlooked him as a possible suspect, eh?"

"I don't think so, Ziz."

"Neither do I, Penny Wise."

THE END

Resurrected Press Mysteries From Louis Tracy

The Albert Gate Mystery

Four men murdered and a fortune in diamonds belonging to the Turkish Sultan stolen, while the Foreign Office official in charge has gone missing. Was it a common jewelry theft or was it a case of international intrigue? This is the question that barrister detective Reginald Brett must solve.

The Bartlett Mystery

When Ronald Tower is murdered on his way to a bridge game on the yacht Sans Souci it at first appears a common crime. But as Rex Carshaw finds, a tragic case of mistaken identity leads to political scandal among the rich and powerful of New York.

The Strange Case of Mortimer Fenley

When the wealthy Mortimer Fenley is struck down by a shot from an express rifle on the steps of his mansion, detectives Winter and Furneaux of Scotland Yard must find the culprit. Was it the artist who claimed he was painting a picture at the time of the shot? The disaffected younger son? Or is there another suspect?

The Stowmarket Mystery

For five generations the Fergus-Hume family has been cursed. Each of the baronets has met a violent end. When the fifth baronet is found slain by a ceremonial Japanese dagger, suspicion falls on his cousin David. It falls to barrister detective Reginald Brett to prove his innocence and find the real murder in a case that spans two continents and as many centuries.

Resurrected Press Mysteries by J. S. Fletcher

The Orange-Yellow Diamond

When an elderly pawnbroker is murdered in the London parish of Paddington, a young, down on his luck writer is accused of the crime. But then it's found the pawnbroker had had in his possession an extraordinary South African diamond worth over eighty-thousand pounds — a diamond that's now missing. It falls to Melky Rubenstein to unravel the mystery and prove the young man's innocence.

The Middle Temple Murder

When an elderly man's body is found on the steps of chambers in the Midde Temple, one of the Inns of Court, it falls to newspaperman Frank Spargo and Detective-Sergeant Rathbury to solve the crime. The murdered man, for indeed it was murder, was found with no money or identification on his person except for a piece of paper with the name and address of a young barrister. Who is the victim? Why was he killed? Who is the murderer?

Scarhaven Keep

Bassett Oliver, the famed actor, has gone missing. When Oliver fails to show for a rehearsal, aspiring playwright Richard Copplestone finds himself sent to the small village of Scarhaven on the northern coast of England to track down the actors movements. What he finds is mystery. Find the answers as Copplestone unravels the mystery of Scarhaven Keep.

Visit www.resurrectedpress.com

Resurrected Press Mysteries by Fergus Hume

The Green Mummy

Professor Braddock hoped to compare the burial practices of the Egyptians with those of the ancient Peruvians with his latest acquisition, the mummy of the last Inca, Caxas. But on arrival, the packing case proved to hold not the mummy, but the body of his assistant Sidney Bolton. It falls to Archie Hope to discover the murderer if he is to marry the professors step-daughter, Lucy Kendal. Who killed Bolton and where is the mummy? Was it the sea captain Hervey? The mysterious Don Pedro? Cockatoo the Polynesian servant? The professor, himself? And what has become of the emeralds? These are the questions that Hope must answer amongst the secrets of the past in The Green Mummy.

The Mystery of a Hansom Cab

"Truth is said to be stranger than fiction, and certainly the extraordinary murder which took place in Melbourne Friday morning goes a long way towards verifying that saying." Thus opens The Mystery of a Hansom Cab, the best selling mystery of the nineteenth century. When a man is found dead in a hansom cab one of Melbourne's leading citizens is accused of the murder. He pleads his innocence, yet refuses to give an alibi. It falls to a determined lawyer and an intrepid detective to find the truth, revealing long kept secrets along the way. Fergus Hume's first and perhaps most famous mystery... The Mystery Of A Hansom Cab.

Visit www.resurrectedpress.com

Resurrected Press Mysteries from the Dr. John Thorndyke Series

Dr. John Thorndyke - Lecturer on Medical Jurisprudence and Forensic Medicine. Before Bones, before CSI, before Quincy, M.E– there was Dr. John Thorndyke solving the most baffling cases of Edwardian London using the latest tools of medical science. Read about his cases in:

The Eye of Osiris
John Bellingham, noted Egyptologist has vanished not once but twice in the same day. Now Dr, Thorndyke must unravel the tangled claims on his estate, solve the riddle of the missing man and find the "Eye of Osiris".

The Mystery of 31 New Inn
When Dr. Jervis is whisked away in a coach with no windows to an unknown location to treat a man in a coma from undivulged causes it is Dr. Thorndyke who must come up with the solution.

The Red Thumb Mark
The first of Dr. Thorndyke's cases finds him trying to prove the innocence of a young man accused of being a diamond thief despite the fact that his finger print was found at the scene of the crime.

John Thorndyke's Cases
More cases of medical mysteries as told by his trusted assistant Jervis, M.D. Eight stories of crime and deduction in Edwardian London.

Visit www.resurrectedpress.com

Resurrected Press Mysteries by John R. Watson & Arthur J. Rees

The Hampstead Mystery

High Court Justice Sir Horace Fewbanks found shot dead in his Hampstead home, a butler with a criminal past, a scorned lover and a hint of scandal. These are the elements of the Hampstead Mystery that Detective Inspector Chippenfield of Scotland Yard must unravel with the assistance of the ambitious Detective Rolfe. But will he be able to sort out the tangled threads of this case and arrest the culprit before he is upstaged by the celebrated gentleman detective Crewe. Follow the details of this amazing case at it plays out across Hampstead, London and Scotland until it reaches a stunning conclusion in the courts of the Old Bailey.

The Mystery of the Downs

When Harry Marsland was caught in a sudden down pour he sought shelter at Cliff Farm. Met at the door by a young woman clearly expecting someone else he is only too glad to get inside to wait out the storm. When they hear a noise upstairs in the deserted house they investigate only to discover the body of the farm's owner, Frank Lumsden, dead of a gunshot wound. Who then, killed Lumsden, and why? Who was the woman expecting and did she have any roll in the murder? These are the questions that private detective Crewe must answer in The Mystery of the Downs.

Visit www.resurrectedpress.com

Other Resurrected Press Mysteries

Mysteries on a Train

Before the Orient Express there was:

The Rome Express by Arthur Griffiths
A man is found dead in his first class sleeping compartment on the express from Rome to Paris. Who was his murderer? The Countess? The English General? His brother the clergy man? The maid who has disappeared? Is the French justice system up to solving the crime? Read about it in The Rome Express.

The Passenger from Calais by Arthur Griffiths
Colonel Basil Annesley finds he is the only passenger on the train from Calais to Lucerne. That is until a mysterious woman shows up at the last minute to book a compartment. Who is after her? What is her secret? Is she a criminal or a victim? Read about it in The Passenger from Calais

Visit us at www.resurrectedpress.com

About Resurrected Press

A division of Intrepid Ink, LLC, Resurrected Press is dedicated to bringing high quality, vintage books back into publication. See our entire catalogue and find out more at www.ResurrectedPress.com.

About Intrepid Ink, LLC

Intrepid Ink, LLC provides full publishing services to authors of fiction and non-fiction books, eBooks and websites. From editing to formatting, from publishing to marketing, Intrepid Ink gets your creative works into the hands of the people who want to read them. Find out more at www.IntrepidInk.com.

www.ingramcontent.com/pod-product-compliance
Lightning Source LLC
Chambersburg PA
CBHW070929180626
46817CB00003B/1221